By the Author of "Handsome Harry."

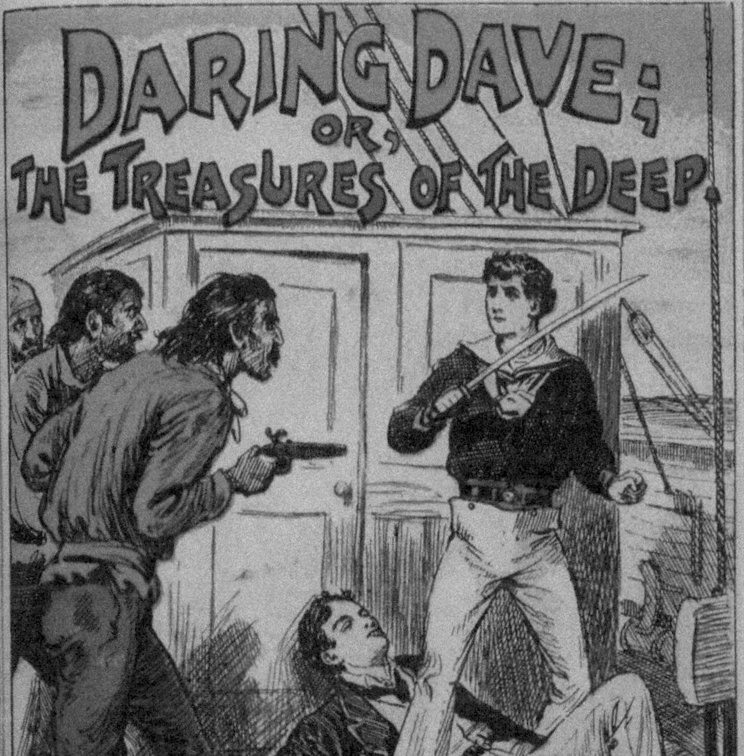

DARING DAVE;
OR,
THE TREASURES OF THE DEEP.

No. 27.   'BEST FOR BOYS" LIBRARY.   3D.

DARING ✳ ✳ DAVE;

OR, THE

TREASURES of the DEEP.

By E. HARCOURT BURRAGE.

DARING DAVE;

OR,

The Treasures of the Deep.

CHAPTER I.

ON BOARD THE WATER SPRITE—A LONELY SEA—
THE BLACK SPECK.

 IT was night upon the sea, far away in the sunny south. Overhead countless stars were gleaming with a brilliancy unknown in the cold, foggy north, no breath of air was stirring, and the wide spread of water just rose and fell like some monster lightly sleeping. Resting on the bosom of the deep was a trim, yacht-like brig, with tall, tapering spars rising above the sails, which hung in loose folds motionless. On deck the watch moved softly to and fro, or rested lazily against the sides of the vessel without exchanging a word.

In the sultry, languid air there was no life. In breathing it there was a lotus-eating effect. All one cared to do was to stand or lie about and think in a pleasant way of nothing in particular.

Early that morning the calm set in, at noon the scorching sun was unendurable and drove the men below or under such shade as the deck afforded ; at night a wonderfully seductive, pleasing languor came over all.

No light was in position to warn passing vessels of the brig's vicinity, for it lay in what was practically an unknown sea.

There was no light aboard, save in the captain's cabin.

There, on a lounge, reclined the commander of the craft, a very young man, not more than twenty-one. He wore a uniform something like that of the English Navy, varying only in two or three respects.

The buttons were different, being plain, save for a small star graven in the centre, and the cut of his coat was less stiff than those worn by our officers at home.

It was open now, owing to the heat, showing a fine silken shirt beneath.

On a table near him was a tumbler half filled with claret and water, in his hand a small, exquisitely flavoured cigar.

Seated by the table, with one elbow on it, and his head upon his hand, was another young fellow, a year or so the junior of the other, and attired in the modest but becoming dress of an ordinary seaman.

The only thing noticeable about it was the fineness of the material, which was of the very best.

The first person was known as Captain Dave, or, as his men called him, Daring Dave, and surname to those under him he had not.

The other was the second in command, " Mr. Fenton " when addressed on deck, in private spoken of by the crew as Fiery Jack, a tribute to his vivacity and dashing style of doing things.

There were two under officers besides, of whom
we shall speak more anon, and a crew of thirty men.

"Thinking, Jack?" said Daring Dave.

"Well—yes—a bit," replied the other, looking up
with a smile. "I can't help looking back sometimes.
It seems hard— But, there, I won't talk about
it."

"Both of us are under a cloud at home," said
Dave, after another silence; "but by-and-bye it
will clear away."

"I suppose such things come right in this world
—sometimes," returned Jack.

"Well, if they don't we won't grieve," replied
Daring Dave. "If good luck should attend our
quest there are hundreds of places on earth where
we can live happily—with money. Anyway, *I* have
enough for us both."

"I thank you, Dave, but it would not do. I am
one of those fools who are sensitive in that respect.
I must spend my own, or spend nothing."

"You are right, Jack," said Dave, with a sigh;
"and there's such a thing as *honour*, which, in the
eyes of some, I have lost; but that I must retrieve
—WILL retrieve ere I am very many years older."

"Well said, Dave!" cried Jack, straightening
himself up. "YOU never give in; but I confess I
did feel a bit down just now. It's this enervating
air, I suppose."

"It is enough, Jack, to send us to sleep for ever.
And I reckon all our fellows are dozing; I don't
hear a movement on board."

"Somebody is coming down the companion, anyway," said Jack, laughing.

"It sounds like Pegs. It is just his dotty way of
walking."

A knock at the door—a soft, insinuating knock—and Daring Dave cried out—

"Come in !"

Then entered Pegs, the second mate—a tall, gaunt-looking man, with the most lugubrious face ever seen above the shoulders of mortal being.

"Well, Pegs, what is it?"

"Curious sound to the north, sir," was the reply.

"What is it like?" asked Dave, as he took a sip of claret.

"Like somebody mortifully wounded—just about to give in," replied Pegs.

"You are generally good at funereal similes, Pegs," remarked Jack.

"Well, sir," replied Pegs, "I gives out such smiles as I've got inside me. A man can't unship a cargo he ain't got in his hold."

"That's true," said Daring Dave, rising. "We will come on deck and hear this wonderful sound. Perhaps it's the wind rising."

"All I've got to say," said Pegs, "is that, if it *is* the wind, it's summat new in that line."

Jack rose at the same time as Dave, and they went out together. Pegs held the door open until they had passed through, and then followed them.

On reaching the deck the two young officers, by the light of the stars, saw the men of the watch in a group on the starboard side of the vessel, every man peering in a northernly direction.

But there was no extraordinary sound to hear, for all was still again.

"Now, Pegs," said Daring Dave, "where's this funereal phenomenon of yours?"

"It *was* over there," answered Pegs, "but it's

collopsed, jest like most curus things when you want 'em to show up."

Bo—o—o—o—o—o !

" There it is again !" cried Pegs.

" Silence, all !" cried Daring Dave.

Boo—o—o—o—o—o !

It was certainly one of the most mournful sounds that ever fell upon the ear of man on land or sea.

It began low, and rose slowly up to a wail, dying gradually away.

" It's like a dog howling," said Pegs ; " but no dog under forty feet high could give us an 'owl like that.   Why, it's miles off."

" It certainly seems far away," said Fiery Jack ; " but in this still air sound will travel far."

" Perhaps, it is a wounded whale, sir ?" suggested one of the watch.

" If you ain't got a better fool's suggestion than *that*, Crupper," said Pegs, " you had better say nothin'."

" Axin' the cap'en and Mister Fenton's parding," said Crupper ; " but whales gits out of their latitude sometimes."

" But they don't come into bilin' seas like this, I reckon," replied Pegs, wrathfully, " they ain't such fools as to go about to find a place to get cooked in."

Bo—o—o—o—

Once more the horrible sound was heard ; but this time it was cut short when it had risen about half way.

It sounded exactly as if somebody had clipped it in two.

" Somebody's cut short his music *this* time," said

And it really seemed so, for the sound was heard no more that night.

They listened for awhile ; but not hearing it again, Daring Dave, after instructing Pegs to watch for any change in the sky, went below, accompanied by Jack.

As soon as they were gone the group broke up, each man walking away to his special post.

"Crupper," said Pegs, sharply.

"Here, sir," replied a little man, as broad as he was long, wheeling sharply round.

"Crupper," said Pegs, "how orfen have I told you not to cut in with your *gab* when me and the captain is in consultation ?"

"I'm a officer," replied Crupper, "and as sich can put in a word now and then."

"Arter me—arter me," said Pegs ; "let that be understood. Cap'en, first mate, second mate, and *then* bo'sun. That's the rotaryation about it."

"The what ?" asked Crupper.

"Rotaryation of it—the sequench. That's the meaning of it. You ain't got no edication, Crupper, and I don't blame you."

"Thank the Lord I ain't got *your* edication," growled Crupper, as he walked away.

CHAPTER II.

A STRANGE VESSEL—IN AMBUSH ON BOARD— THE FIGHT AND THE VICTORY.

EARILY the hot night passed away, no welcome breeze rising to cool the heated air.

In due time a copper-coloured sun peeped above the horizon, revealing the grace and beauty of Daring Dave's vessel—the Water Sprite.

Pegs' watch had been changed, and Fiery Jack was now in charge of the deck.

With a glow of joy he cast his eyes upon his surroundings, which were well calculated to make young blood flow freely.

The Water Sprite was no pleasure-going vessel, but a well-fitted little cruiser, with five steel guns, that gleamed in the morning light.

From her water-line to the top of her masts she had the look of a smart little craft, which could, if need be, become a veritable ocean bee or wasp.

The men were armed as they would be in the navy in the time of war, and at Jack's side hung a sword in a scabbard of the finest steel, that shone like silver.

He wore a belt made to carry revolvers, but at the time had not those world-wide weapons about him.

From contemplation of the craft Jack's attention was drawn to one of the men of the watch, who uttered an exclamation and pointed northward.

Following the direction of his hand, Jack saw a vessel about two miles away with a general troubled look about her canvas not to be accounted for in the ordinary way.

But how came that vessel there?

She had certainly not been within sight the night before, and it was barely possible that a breeze could have brought her thither without the Water Sprite having at least had a breath of it.

"Go down to the captain," said Jack; "ask him if he can come on deck and bring his glass with him."

The man touched his forelock and disappeared. Fiery Jack, leaning on the vessel's side, shaded his eyes with his hands.

He had good eyesight, and although far away, he could make out that she had the appearance of being a deserted vessel. Her canvas and ropes were all in disorder like some person's hair blown about by a high wind.

In three minutes Daring Dave was on deck, bringing his binoculars with him.

"What is it, Jack?" he asked.

"A case of desertion, I think," was the reply. "Have a look at her?"

Dave raised his eyebrows slightly as he saw the disordered vessel, and having sighted his glasses, he took a long and steady look at her.

"Deserted," he said.

"Just my opinion," replied Jack; "but why?"

"Mutiny is at the bottom of it, I expect," replied Daring Dave. "Suppose we go and have a look at her. There's no chance of a breeze springing up," with a glance at the sky. "Half-a-dozen men will take us there and back in the gig before breakfast."

It was something to do, and a little natural curiosity was also at the bottom of the idea. So having had Pegs called up, the gig was lowered, and with half-a-dozen men, Daring Dave and Fiery Jack were rowed in the direction of the strange craft.

As they drew near they saw that two boats were moored against the side, which made the affair stranger still. As for the disorder in the rigging, it became every minute more and more apparent.

Not a living creature was to be seen on board. Her appearance was that of a vessel that had been roughly hauled over and deserted.

At length they were within a few yards of her, and more evidence of foul work having been done was discovered.

All about the vessel, keeping company with it in the calm sea, were wine-cases, papers off champagne-bottles, straw, and odds and ends of male and female wearing apparel.

"Mutiny for a dead certainty !" said Daring Dave. "Steady there, men. Hold on with the hook ! Once more, steady !"

Seizing a piece of rope that was dangling over the side, he clambered up on board. Jack followed him with all speed, and was just in time to receive the shock of a terrible surprise.

A dozen ruffians, who had been lying in conceal-ment, sprung up and rushed at Daring Dave, who had barely drawn his sword, which, like Jack, he carried at his side, when he was struck down by a belaying-pin hurled at him.

The ruffians, who were of the swarthy Malay type of face, were all armed with knives and some with pistols ; with a yell they rushed in a body at Fiery Jack, who, with flashing eyes, whipped out his sword and standing up boldly by his fallen captain, prepared to defend both or die.

The foremost ruffian aimed a pistol at his head, but as he fired it Jack gave him a slash across the arm, which disturbed his aim and disabled him.

"Water Sprites to the rescue !" cried Jack.

The gallant fellows in the boat needed no urging.

At first, too utterly amazed by the sudden tumult to do anything, they speedily realised that something was wrong, and came tumbling up on deck like so many little billows of humanity, each man as he arrived dashing headlong—sword in hand—at the brawny ruffians.

Jack had already accounted for two, who lay upon the deck mortally wounded, each by a dexterous thrust through the breast.

"Hurrah ! Good Water Sprites !" cried Jack, as with a resistless dash he went right into the thick of the foe, who scattered wildly, fighting for their lives.

"Keep them up in the bows, away from the captain !" cried Jack. "At them, lads ! No quarter ! Down with them, or tumble them into the sea !"

"Hurrah for Fiery Jack !" cried one of the men, forgetting in the excitement of the moment the respect due to an officer.

It was a slip of the tongue, which Jack remembered afterwards, but not in a resentful spirit. The guilty one was never so much as reproved for it.

It was a wild fight while it lasted, but coolness and courage soon made it a complete victory.

Barring a few cuts—" notches " the sailors called them—and a bullet in the fleshy part of one of the men's thighs—he afterwards picked it out with his pocket-knife—the Water Sprites suffered no injury.

But for the dozen ruffians there was no quarter, and short and sharp was the measure of punishment dealt out to them.

" We'll kill 'em first, and ask 'em their bissness arterwards !" cried one of the Water Sprites, and the little joke actually drew laughter from his messmates.

Foremost throughout was Fiery Jack, with that terrible sword, as swift and unerring in its death-dealing as the lightning flash.

Down went the foe one after the other until only one remained, and he took refuge in the bowsprit.

Thither Fiery Jack, roused to a dangerous fever heat, followed him, regardless of a revolver aimed at his head.

A wild aim, a drawn trigger, a bullet flying uselessly over his head, one thrust of the sword, and all was over.

With a gasp the last of the foe let go his hold and fell into the sea.

There, one of those undertakers of the ocean, a shark, was awaiting him, or, indeed, anybody else who might happen to come in its way.

The uncanny brute turned on its back, opened its jaws, snapped them to, and dived with its horrible breakfast under the sea.

" I don't want to see THAT again," thought Jack, as he jumped lightly back on deck to his quickly breathing men. " You have done well, my brave fellows, and now we must see to— Hullo ! who the deuce is this ?"

Well might he ask the question, for, head and shoulders out of the hatchway of the hold, was as strange a figure as ever was seen on shipboard.

It was a stout man with a very red nose, spectacles and attired in a smoking-cap and dressing-gown.

In his arms he held an enormous trombone.

Fiery Jack cast one glance at him, then at Daring Dave, who, with rather a bewildered look upon his face, was now rising to his feet.

Then he looked at the strange apparition again, asking himself if he were not the victim of a nightmare in the daytime.

As for the sailors, they were staring at the figure too, and one of them, breathing hard, exclaimed—

"I'm blessed if they ain't got waxwork figgers aboard."

And very much like one was the wearer of the smoking-cap, as with a stolid face he slowly stared around at the scene on deck, at Daring Dave, Fiery Jack, the sailors, and the dead and dying ruffians.

At last, just as Jack mechanically offered his hand o his captain, the mysterious stranger put the mouthpiece of the trombone to his lips, and blew hard and long until his head appeared to be double its natural size and the veins of his forehead swelled almost to bursting—

Bo-o-o-o-o-o-o-o-o !

CHAPTER III.

A STARTLING STORY—SEARCHING THE VESSEL.

ANG me !". exclaimed one of the sailors, "if it ain't the dying grampus we heerd last night."

Of this there could be little doubt, for the sound was absolutely the same, although, being heard so near, its volume was overpowering.

But the musician was evidently satisfied with his performance.

A broad, complacent smile expanded his face as he mounted slowly to the deck.

" I gif you a tune," he said, "so to honare victoree. Shall I gif you more ?"

" For goodness' sake, no !" replied Jack. "Dave, how do you feel ?"

" A bit woolly about the head," was the reply ; " but I am coming round. I am not much hurt."

He cast a quick glance round the deck, and giving Jack a friendly pat upon the shoulders, added—

" I see you have done very well without me ; but who are these vagabonds ?"

" Perhaps our friend here can enlighten us," said Fiery Jack. "I say, old fellow, what is the name

"It ze maxim of my life to see all and nothing say," replied the stranger, with great deliberation. "Her name am ze Colorada Eagle."

"An American?"

"It am zo; but as I nevare—"

"But these men are surely not the crew?"

"Zey VAS. Ah! it is a sad story, but not for me to tell. You make up a great victoree, and, vid your leaf, I vunce more play a tune."

"I beg of you not to do so—at present," said Daring Dave.

"Vat, you got no ear for musick?"

"No, not much."

"It is a pity, I am all music. Ze spirit of Vagnare am on me. I play all tunes. Ze idle fool laugh, but let zem vait until zey hear my great opera 'Ze Vinkle and ze Vhale.'"

His manner of speaking was very slow, and all round he was a very deliberate person. Fiery Jack, turning to Dave, said—

"It's no use questioning him further now, is it?"

"You might ask him his name," suggested Dave.

On being asked for his name the stranger groped about in one of the pockets of his dressing-gown, and presently fished out a soiled card. Jack took it and read—

"VUNDER FULE,

. *"Cook and Composer of Musick."*

"Hanged if I know what to make of the fellow," said Jack. "He certainly doesn't look like one of the murderous gang we have laid low. However, we must talk to him by-and-bye."

The first thing to be done was to dispose of the

dead with as little ceremony as possible, and assistance arriving in the form of Crupper with half a score of men, the task was at once entered upon.

Crupper explained that the fight had been observed on board the Water Sprite, and by the command of Pegs he had come to give assistance.

"We were afraid, sir, as you were overweighted," he said to the captain. "Not as *I* had any doubts about the issoo."

The deck was speedily cleared of the men who had fallen, one only being now alive.

He was a swarthy fellow, an Indian half-breed, grizzled with age, who was taking his defeat and prospect of immediate death with a stoic's resignation.

He signed to Daring Dave and Fiery Jack to come to him, indicating that he had something to say.

Knowing how cunning and treacherous his race at a pinch could be, they approached him watchfully, in case he had a weapon concealed and meditated mischief.

But he had no such intent, and there was almost a kindly gleam in his eye as he glanced from one to the other.

Dave had now almost recovered from the effect of the blow he received, and, beyond being rather pale, there was nothing to show that he had recently received a blow that had stretched him insensible upon the deck.

"See here, you two—brave—strong—handsome," said the half-caste, "me something to say; but make haste, as I go to my fathers."

"Can we do anything for you?" asked Daring Dave, kindly enough.

He could be generous to a fallen foe, no matter how vile and treacherous he may have been.

"No, nothing," was the answer. "Life go away—listen, you two brave and strong—hear Wapita, who tell you to go and fight the Nevada Tiger—him who is called by his people Osric Grame."

"Who is he—and where shall I find him?" asked Daring Dave, willing to humour what he considered to be the fancy of a dying man.

A vivid light flamed up in the eyes of the half-caste.

With an effort he lifted himself up half-way to a sitting position and pointed south.

"There—there," he said. "You will find him among the Many Islands. He is a great thief, but others rob for him. Ah! he send out men. 'Go join ship,' he say, 'work as a sailor. Then wait. At night rise up, kill crew, captain, passengers—bring ship to me.' It done much—too much."

"Impossible!" exclaimed Daring Dave.

"It true!" said the dying Wapita, with a wonderful vehemence, when his dying state is considered. "It must be done. Hear me—it done—captain glad of men—take all—any whom—so soft spoken all—no sign—no word—but one night all ready—only a few blows and all over. The ship taken—what then? She sail away to the Many Islands, and is seen no more. What of that? She not come home, Ah! Lost at sea—go down in storm—strike iceberg, the fools say—but they not know. Osric Grame among the islands—laugh—make merry—it is all true."

He stopped suddenly and fell back heavily, as if struck down by a blow. The light in his eyes was fading fast, and he was breathing heavily.

They spoke to him; but he did not answer. All he did was to raise his hand a few inches and point southward.

His lips were moving; but Jack, who bent over him to catch any possible utterance, could not hear a word. Only the first signs of the coming death-rattle escaped from between the parted lips.

A few moments more and he was gone.

What was the nature of the impulse that led him to tell such an awful story it was impossible to say. But he had told it, and the question was—could it be true?

In searching over the ship abundant evidence of mutiny and murder were found.

Bloodstains and other indications of deadly struggles were found in every cabin, and the ship's papers, log, and books that could serve to give a clue to her had been destroyed.

There was a small cabin for passengers, and in it they found a handful of woman's hair of a golden colour, torn from the head of some hapless creature who had fallen a prey to the atrocious ruffians who had at last paid the penalty of their crimes.

In the hold was a cargo of wines, silks, and other products of the European Continent to the value of many thousand pounds.

Part of it had been rummaged over, and the number of broken cases bore witness to the fact that the mutineers had been drinking heavily.

"The story is true," said Daring Dave, as he and Jack ascended to the deck, "and you and I, Jack, have a congenial task before us."

"It suits me to a hair," replied Jack, with a glow-ing cheek. "We must unearth this Osric Grame

" I wonder—if—" began Daring Dave, and then he stopped.

" You wonder—if—" said Jack.

" No—it cannot be," rejoined Dave ; " it was only a passing thought.   There is a mystery in connection with my own life that I should like to fathom ; but it is not probable that this Osric Grame can have anything to do with it."

" Who knows ?" said Jack.   " Things in this world come about most strangely."

" We know nothing of the man as yet," said Daring Dave.   " Wait until we have found his stronghold and rooted out something of his life— then I may, perhaps, try to piece the fragments of my early life together.   It is strange that they should flash upon me now, and in the midst of them a face I have never seen, which I feel sure is that of Osric Grame."

He spoke hurriedly, and, as if anxious to have done with the subject for the time, ran up to the deck. Jack followed him with a step as light as that of a schoolboy.

What a prospect of adventure was before him !

It did, indeed, " suit him to a hair," for he was made of the stuff which gives to the world its most heroic spirits.

The men had not been idle during their leader's absence.   The mop and the bucket had been employed about the deck, and most of the signs of the recent conflict had been cleared away.

The dead had been given to the sea, and barrels and things upset during the struggle put in order.

Vunder Fule was busy making up a small bundle which he said was his luggage.   It consisted of a manuscript of his opera, the "Vinkle and the Vhale."

The latter was tied up and closely sealed so as to be kept from prying eyes.

"By-em-bye," he said to one of the sailors, "some great managare of teatre sez to me 'Vere is your great opera?' I sez to him, 'Behold it!' Zen he take ze manscript, and sez to de musicians, 'Learn dis.' Dey learn it, and de public come to hear it."

"Well, if the whole opera is anything like that bit you gave us last night and this morning," said the sailor, "the company will want a drop o' spirits to save 'em from busting."

"Vat I play to you," said Vunder Fule, serenely, "are de firse bar ob zat opera. It catch de ear in a moment."

"As far as I felt it," replied the sailor, "it seemed to catch my innards."

The reappearance of Daring Dave and his lieutenant on deck cut short the conversation.

Orders were given for the vessel to be left exactly as she was, nothing to be taken away.

The only thing done was to lash the helm so that when a breeze sprung up she could go steadily before it.

And then they left her to the mercy of wind and wave.

Although Daring Dave might very fairly have helped himself to a portion of her cargo he was too proud and honest to do so.

"I leave to others," he said, "the task of plundering a helpless vessel."

On their way back to the Water Sprite a few questions were put to Vunder Fule which elicited the information that the Eagle was an American vessel trading between New York and Marseilles.

Vunder Fule took a berth at the latter place, his intention being to go to New York, where he hoped his ability as a cook and talent as a musician would bring him a fortune.

It was his gift as a cook that saved his life when the mutineers rose up and killed everybody else on board.

There was no doubt it was a preconcerted thing, because the men were well-treated by the captain, the food was good, and the duties light, owing to the favourable breezes.

Here was another confirmation of the story of the dying half-caste.

Vunder Fule was affected to tears when he spoke of the passengers who had been murdered.

There were eight of them—six men, "good fellows," he declared, and a mother and daughter.

The latter were going out to join the husband and father, who had been some years abroad endeavouring to make a fortune.

He found it at last and wrote for them to join him in the new country.

Joyously they were going thither when their horrible fate overtook them.

"It vas so bad," said Vunder Fule, "zat I veep all night. Oh! zey shrieks and zey cry. 'Mercy—mercy!' But zer vas no mercy in de hearts of der beasts. Oh! but for my vriend here"—patting his trombone—"I surely die."

These details, brief as they were, sufficed to fire the blood of the listeners, and when the story was re-told to those who had remained on board the Water Sprite, a great cry for vengeance went up

Daring Dave called his men together, and told them of his projected search for Osric Grame. They shouted and waved their caps in wild enthusiasm.

"Captain, we are with you," they cried, and then once more the favourite name of their leader was heard.

"Hurrah for Daring Dave—Hurrah !"

CHAPTER IV.

UPON THE SEA—THAT TROMBONE—A TRIP ACROSS THE ISLAND.

GAILY the Water Sprite sped over the dancing waves before a splendid breeze. Every inch of can-vas was set, and, like a race-horse urged on by whip and spur, she raced along.

The light-hearted men could feel her *throb* with every bound as if she were indeed a thing of life.

A sharp look-out was kept for any chance vessel or a sight of land ; but since they met with the deserted vessel two days before, not a speck of any sort on the broad bosom of the waters had been seen.

There was only one unhappy man on board, and that was Vunder Fule. He was not allowed to play his trombone during the day, and only for five minutes after sunset.

It might be music that he extracted from that majestic instrument, but it was not the sort of melody which anyone on board could appreciate. In vain the musician pleaded with tears in his

'Ze Vinkle and ze Vhale.'" Pegs, on behalf of the officers, and Crupper, as spokesman for the men, said—" No."

"Zen I pine avay," said Vunder Fule. "I cannot lif vithout musick."

As they did not wish him to die, for he proved to be a first-rate cook, he was allowed to indulge himself five minutes after sunset, as before stated.

While the melody was being poured forth, everybody stopped their ears, but they could not by any means shut out the dolorous sounds. All they could do was to soften them down.

"I never heard anything like it, sir," said Pegs to Fiery Jack. "I've heard a whole menagerie roaring at once, but it was nothing to it."

"Perhaps he may lose the trombone one day," said Jack, significantly.

"It's never out of his sight," replied Pegs; "he even takes it into his hammock and holds it tight in his arms."

"Well, he is useful as a cook," was all Jack could say.

It was the evening of the second day, and the thoughts of all on board were on the impending musical suffering.

In a quarter of an hour Vunder Fule would be at liberty to blow his soul for five minutes into the big brass tube, and he was standing by the cuddy, screwing the mouthpiece up tight and fondling it as a mother does her child.

Crupper was standing close by, watching his movements with a visage expressive of the utmost disgust.

"I say, mister," he said, "don't you think you could hold orf for one night?"

"Oh ! no," sighed Vunder Fule. "I no sleep without him. Music is my draught of sleep."

"It'll be a sleeping-draught for a lot of us if you don't go easy with it," growled Crupper, "for I'm blessed if I don't think some of us will sink under it. If you could play the British 'ornpipe on it, it wouldn't matter so much, but the stuff you turns out is like the groans of helephants dying on the battle-field."

"Oh ! no, sir," said Vunder Fule, "you haf not ze soul of melody."

Crupper was about to say something very uncom-plimentary about melody when the look-out cried in ringing tones—

"Land-ho !"

Daring Dave, who was seated aft smoking a a cigar with Fiery Jack, sprang to his feet.

"Where away ?" he cried.

"Sou'-west by west, sir."

Daring Dave picked up his glass, which was lying upon the deck, and rapidly sighted it for the horizon sou'-west by west.

A line of dots of various sizes lay spread out before his view.

"It's the Many Islands, Jack," he said.

"Which further confirms the half-caste's story," replied Jack.

As the Water Sprite was going south the helm was put up so as to bring her head in the direction of the islands.

This gave her the wind on the beam, and she heeled over so that her leeward lower yards almost reached the water.

Vunder Fule, not being prepared for the change, fell forward with his instrument, which struck the deck with the noise of cymbals, and rolled into the scuppers.

Vunder Fule slid down after it, and, with a wail, picked up the trombone and examined it with an anxious face.

"Lord send it is burst!" muttered Crupper, and it may be said that his utterance found an echo in the hearts of all on deck.

But apparently it was unhurt, for Vunder Fule blew a short sharp note out of it that was like the yelp of a monster dog.

"It am safe," he said, looking around with an expansive smile.

Shortly after the sun went down, and by that time the islands were clearly in view to the eye. Vunder Fule had his five minutes of melody, accompanied by the muttered execrations of the listeners, and then retired for the night.

In a little while darkness was on the sea.

Being near land, Daring Dave sent a man into the chains to heave the lead, and the sound of his voice as he gave his report sounded short and sharp on the night air.

The sob of the sea against the sides of the vessel, and the occasional creaking of a block, were the only other sounds that broke the stillness.

At length the cry of the man heaving the lead became of importance.

"Ten fathoms three—ten fathoms two—eight fathoms!"

"All hands to shorten sail!" cried Daring Dave.

In less than a minute the ratlines were dotted with men going aloft. Half a minute more the speed of the Water Sprite slackened.

"Eight fathoms five—*seven*—SIX!"

Pegs was at the helm, and, in obedience to a word from his captain, brought the vessel round right in the eye of the wind.

Then the anchor was dropped, the sails furled, and she was at rest for the night.

The islands were still about two miles away, and it was pretty certain that the Water Sprite had been brought to anchor on a sand bank ; and there were breakers ahead, for the waves, as they beat upon the shore, could be plainly heard.

The night passed and the morning came again— a brilliant day, with a soft, refreshing breeze.

Each watch reported no light or fire or any sign of life on shore, and when Daring Dave with his glass examined the coast he found nothing to indicate the presence of man.

Before them lay an island of several miles in width, and to the right and left many more were visible, the furthermost being mere specks.

The appearance of the nearest island was very promising, for it had rising hills and plenty of wood about it.

After breakfast Daring Dave, with Pegs and half-a-dozen men, got ready to go ashore. The line of breakers ahead had gaps here and there, and no difficulty in getting ashore was anticipated.

Fiery Jack watched them until they were through the breakers, and then turned his attention to the sea on the right and left.

Possibly there might be natives who would naturally come out in their canoes to look at the strange vessel.

But no craft of any description appeared in sight, and in two hours Daring Dave was back again.

" It's a bigger island than we thought, Jack," he

said ; " this is the narrow end of it.   There's quite a mountain on the farther side.   I tell you, old fellow, we've just got to explore it.   It's the monarch of the group."

" No sign of natives or of Osric Grame ?"

" None ; but for all that they may be there. However, I mean to start at once and cross it."

" Then I must go with you."

" Well, Jack, suppose you and I go ?   Pegs can take care of the Sprite."

They set out as arranged, and struck across the island, taking a bee-line to a fair-sized, smooth-faced mountain on the other side.

Night by that time was upon them, and the two friends very quietly went to rest on the bare ground.

The day had been very hot, and the night was warm, without dew.

They, therefore, suffered no inconvenience.

They discovered that the island was well watered and abounded in fruit and small game.

There were also some wild hogs, the presence of which was not easily accounted for.

In the morning they clambered up the mountain, and at a high elevation (they did not go to the top) closely surveyed the country with Dave's binoculars.

No sign of human being could they find.

"The islands are here," said Daring Dave, with a sigh ; " but Osric Grame is not.   Either we have come to the wrong place or the story is a myth."

" A few days ashore will be welcome to the men," suggested Jack, "and there is plenty of shooting for you and me."

"We will have two quiet days here," assented Dave.

CHAPTER V.

ON THE ISLE—SAVED BY A TROMBONE—TWO
INNOCENTS FROM THE SEA—BETTER, PERHAPS
THEY HAD BEEN DROWNED.

HE next day Vunder Fule sat within a tent erected about a mile from the shore.

He was alone and sound asleep.

Outside, beneath a tree, Daring Dave had lain himself down to rest, and fallen asleep, too, for the day was sultry to oppressiveness.

A third of the crew were ashore, scattered about and bent on enjoying themselves, as Jack Tars always do the instant they set foot on land.

Fiery Jack, as restless a youngster as ever drew breath, had declined to join his captain in a siesta, and had gone away into a wood in search of game.

As Vunder Fule slept he snored, and the sound attracted Crupper, who was moving about some distance off.

He was an officer, and could not fraternise with the men.

Therefore, he was alone, Pegs, his only possible companion, being on board.

Crupper heard the snoring, and, advancing softly to the tent, peeped in.

There was Vunder Fule sound asleep on his back, and the wonderful trombone by his side, not in his arms as when he slept on board.

A malicious twinkle lightened Crupper's eyes.

" I'll give him a job to get music out of it to-night," he muttered.

Like a stealthy Indian bent on scalping a sleeping foe, he crawled into the tent, got possession of the precious instrument, and stole out with it.

Having collected a lot of pieces of sticks, several stones and leaves, he jammed them into the mouth of the trombone so as to effectually close its throttle, and then, more stealthily than before, replaced it.

Having successfully accomplished this crime, he made off as fast as his little legs would carry him, and vanished from the scene.

Strange to say, the moment he was gone Vunder Fule ceased to snore.

He suddenly left a stormy sea, and floated in still waters.

And thus he slept on for a little while.

Then he suddenly awoke as if somebody had stricken him.

But he was alone in the tent.

It was so very strange that in some trepidation he sprang up into a sitting position.

His first thought was of his trombone.

It was quite safe, and he softly chuckled.

" Ah ! my child," he said, softly, as he patted it, " I forget you for one moment.   I neglect you."

He fondled it tenderly, and a longing to blow just *one* note upon it took possession of him.

He put it to his lips ; but did no more, for a harsh noise was heard without the tent.

"I tell you, sir, that we've got to get rid o' this lot somehow. They ain't here for pleasure."

"Hadn't we better ask the cap'en what to do?" enquired another voice, oily and low.

"And get cursed for wasting time! No. Look you. There's the boss of the craft. If we settle him—"

The blood of Vunder Fule froze in his veins.

The voices were strange to him, and he was certain the speakers did not belong to the Water Sprite.

Rising, he walked softly to the mouth of the tent and peeped forth.

He saw two raffish-looking sailors, very different to the trim fellows of the Water Sprite, stealthily, rifle in hand, approaching his sleeping captain.

One, in addition to his rifle, had a knife, and the intention of the pair was obvious.

They meant to assassinate Daring Dave—quietly with the knife if he remained asleep, or shoot him down if he awoke.

An ordinary person would have uttered a warning cry; not so Vunder Fule, who in some things was extraordinarily gifted.

His thoughts flew to his trombone, and he placed the mouthpiece to his lips.

His first effort to blow was futile; the "stuffing" supplied by Crupper stopped the way.

But Vander Fule, not to be denied, put on full power with startling effect.

Out flew the leaves and rubbish as from a volcano, accompanied by such a roar as never before was blown out of any musical instrument.

What the two raffish seamen thought of it exactly we cannot say, but they were scared.

the other leaped into the air as if he had received a smart cut from a whip.

At that moment Daring Dave awoke and jumped to his feet, seizing his rifle as he did so.

Instinctively scenting danger, he cocked his weapon, and his eye alighting on the two staggered ruffians, he covered them.

" Stand !" he cried, " or I fire. "

The fallen man made no attempt to rise ; the other stood still, with a cowed look upon his face.

" Drop your weapons !" was the next command.

Just for a moment they hesitated ; but a slight movement of Dave's rifle, as if he were taking closer aim, caused them to change their views about resistance.

The knife and rifles were thrown to the ground, and Daring Dave, lowering his weapon, walked up to within a few feet of them.

" If you attempt to stir without permission," he said, " I will shoot you down. What are you doing here ?"

" Nothin' but just looking around," replied the man still upon his feet.

Vunder Fule, who, by his mighty effort to clear the trombone, had fairly blown all the air out of his body, stood up to this point gasping like a thoroughly-breathed runner.

Now he managed to get out a few words—

" Lie ! You going to kill—captain."

" Oh ! indeed," said Daring Dave. " And you gave me warning ?"

" Zey stop up ze trombone," replied Vunder Fule ; " but zey not know vat a player I am. I git dem out—everyting."

instrument before!" said the man who had previously spoken. "We was just a-walking around, as I said, when we heard a roar that was like the trumpeting of a herd of elephants."

"Who are you?" said Daring Dave, quickly.

"My name's Aaron Nozzle, and my partner is Waydown Bubbs," answered the man.

"What are you?"

"'Merican sailors—shipwrecked."

"On this island?"

"No—leagues from here," said Aaron Nozzle; "wasn't we, Waydown?"

"We was," replied Waydown Bubbs. "Mayn't I get up, mister?"

"Yes," replied Daring Dave, curtly. "How did you get here?"

"We came in an open boat," returned Nozzle; "didn't we, Waydown? Speak the truth, if you bust in doing it."

"In—a—open boat, if I die for it," said Bubbs.

"We was only strollin' around," said Aaron Nozzle "and naturally, being in a strange country, we were ready for action if need be. But as for a-harming anybody—why, snakes alive!—what do you take us for?"

"Keep where you are for a minute," said Daring Dave. "Pick up those weapons, Vunder Fule, if you please."

While the great musician was engaged in this work the two would-be assassins eyed him with a malevolence rarely expressed by the human countenance.

Daring Dave quietly observed their looks, and made a few mental notes thereon. As Vunder Fule accomplished his task some of the seamen came straggling in, among them Crupper, who had heard that fearful blast upon the trombone, and came back marvelling at the lung power of the performer.

"Take these men on board," said Daring Dave, "and ask Mr. Pegs to keep them in close custody until I am on board."

"Keep ze villains tight," cried Vunder Fule, who, with one eye closed, was endeavouring to get a view of the inside of the trombone, with the object of finding out if that most precious instrument had received any damage. "Zey stuff all dis rubbish into my beautiful child. Zee here, Mr. Crupper—here it am—all round."

"Mercy on us!" exclaimed Crupper, with a face expressive of blank dismay. "How could they have the heart to do it! Here, come along, you two, whoever you be, an' wheersoever you come from. This is a serus thing. It's the most unnateral thing I ever heerd on. Stuff up a beautiful tootler like that! Why, murder's light fooling to it."

There were about half-a-dozen men besides Crupper now assembled, all staring at the strangers, and wondering where on earth they came from.

But they were too well disciplined to ask questions, and falling in round the two prisoners, they escorted them down to the sea, Vunder Fule, by the direction of Daring Dave, accompanying them.

He followed behind, reviling the two strangers for their daring attempt to "nobble" his trombone, stopping now and then to test its present state of efficiency by extracting a short, sharp note from it.

Crupper played chorus to his revilings by expressing his horror at the audacity of the attempt, and the genuineness of his indignation can be measured by the reader who is in the secret as to the true author of that serious business.

But when Vunder Fule came to a declaration about the attempt on the life of the captain, Crupper became truly concerned, and, shaking his fist at the ashen-faced captives, he cried—

"Blarm you both! If that's proved to be true I'll run a rope up to the yard-arm and turn you off myself."

"Well, it ain't proved yet," said Aaron Nozzle, with an attempt at bravado. "Don't get excited."

"Seems to me," added Waydown Bubbs, "that we'd better ha' been drowned at sea than fallen among these ere people."

Perhaps it would have been better for both him and his companion if they had indeed found a resting-place under the sea.

CHAPTER VI.

THE FIRST SHOT—A GALLANT RESCUE.

HAVING seen the men with their charges well on the way, Daring Dave flung his rifle over his back and proceeded with the agility of a practised climber to ascend an adjacent tree.

Having gone as high as the branches permitted, he carefully scanned the coast to the right and left.

He could see a few of his men lounging among the rocks and smoking their pipes, and larking and chatting together. Seaward lay the Water Sprite, with her canvas close furled, and that was all.

Inland, his view was restricted by other trees in his immediate vicinity, and he soon descended again to terra firma.

"Those vagabonds have lied. There is no other boat but mine to be seen."

Who then were these men?

Were they some of the tools employed by Osric Grame—if such a person existed—in mutiny and piracy on the high seas?

These were questions which could not be answered just then, and he resolved to await the return of Fiery Jack.

In half an hour that lively young lieutenant returned with half-a-dozen wild birds he had shot in his hand. When he heard of the discovery of the two strangers he was not much surprised.

"I have found evidence of others being here," he said. "There is a distinct trail of men going to and fro in the wood. I also picked up these."

He took out of his pocket half-a-dozen empty rifle cartridges, which, apparently, had been fired within a few days.

Daring Dave examined them, and found the well-known name of "Ely, Maker," stamped upon the metal end.

"Jack," he said, "we must not allow the men to straggle any more. We must communicate with the Water Sprite, and signal for them to come back."

They struck the tent, rolled it up, and it being a light one, Jack shouldered it, and they strolled back to the sea.

The ground being open they did not fear a foe,

but Daring Dave nevertheless kept a sharp look-out.

In safety they reached the shore, and shortly after the boat which had taken Nozzle and Bubbs on board returned.

It had just grounded on the shore, when two shots were heard in the direction of the rocks, and several of the men were seen running towards them.

Daring Dave hastened to meet them. They came panting up, crying—

" Get aboard, captain ! There's a swarm of piratical thieves coming down upon us !"

" Steady, men ; we cannot desert our comrades," replied Daring Dave.

" All right, sir," replied one of the men ; " they are coming in."

Stragglers were now seen hastening in the direction of the boat, casting quick glances behind them as they ran.

Half-a-dozen shots rattled out one after the other.

" How many are there ashore ?" asked Daring Dave.

" Thirteen, sir."

"An unlucky number, if there is such a thing. Here they come. Two—three—four—five—six—seven."

" Two more on the right, sir."

" That's nine—ten—eleven—twelve—"

The men appeared in sight as he spoke, and anxious eyes were cast around for the thirteenth.

As the direction he had taken was not known, it was impossible to go to his assistance. All they could do was to wait for him.

" When were you attacked ?" asked Daring Dave.

"We were just moving about," replied one of the men, "when I see some heads pop up over a rock. I calls out to my messmates to get together, but we hadn't no time. Up jumps a whole regiment of 'em, right along in a broken line about two hundred yards away. They fired a shot, and we cleared out, captain—if you'll forgive us."

"Quite right," said Daring Dave; "there was no need for you to stand still and be shot down like rabbits. But where is the thirteenth man?"

"There he is!" cried Fiery Jack. "Look—ahead —turning out of the wood!"

All eyes were turned in the direction he pointed. Out of the wood where Jack had recently been shooting dashed a sailor, cutlass in hand.

As soon as he was in the open he turned and let fly into the bush with his revolver. Then out leaped four swarthy ruffians, armed with knives, who spread themselves out with the object of surrounding him.

"Stay here," cried Daring Dave to his men, as he dashed forward.

"I must come with you," said Fiery Jack.

"Go back!" cried Dave.

"I can't. I must be in it."

"Go back—I *command* you—for the sake of the rest."

When Daring Dave spoke in such a decided fashion he was not to be disobeyed, and Fiery Jack, making a wry face, stopped short.

"All right, old fellow," he muttered; "the next time I will get the start of YOU."

Watched by his followers with admiration, not unmingled with anxiety, Daring Dave sped over the ground like a hare in the direction of his follower—

a young sailor not more than eighteen years of age. He was but a boy, but he had pluck. Keeping his face to the foe, and his cutlass poised to strike a blow, he dashed, with a light step, towards the sea.

The four tigerish-looking ruffians followed him up, closing in with a rapidity that would have soon been fatal to him.

Absorbed in their deadly purpose, they neither saw nor heard Daring Dave approach until he was within twenty yards of them.

Then one caught sight of him and uttered a yell of warning to the others.

Mad with the prospect of losing their prey, they all rushed in, and a wild struggle took place between them and the young sailor.

He slashed one ruffian across the face, and sent him blind and bleeding to the earth. Then he, in turn, received a blow from a knife in the back, which laid him in the dust.

In another moment the blow would have been repeated again and again from the merciless rascals, but Daring Dave was upon them.

Like a whirlwind he came to the rescue.

First a shot, mere guesswork as to aim, bowled one over, and the butt of the weapon laid another upon the ground, oblivious of all around him.

The fourth made a wild and futile stab at Dave, and then turned and fled.

"Can you get up?" asked Daring Dave of the fallen sailor.

"I'll try, sir," he answered; and he made an effort to do so, but he fell back with a groan.

"All the life is running out of me, sir," he said. "Don't risk your life by stopping here with me.

There's others coming on through the wood—a swarm of 'em."

" I can't leave you here, my good fellow," said Daring Dave. " Now, let us see."

He put his arm around the lad and raised him up, but he could not stand. The blood was flowing in a regular stream from the wound, and a deadly faintness had come over him.

" I'm a dying, sir. Don't stop here, I beg of you, sir," he said, faintly.

" I *won't* leave you," said Daring Dave. "You are not so heavy, my lad ; I think I can carry you."

Here yells were heard in the wood, and once more the wounded youth implored his captain to leave him.

" It's throwing your life away, sir," he said.

Daring Dave's answer was to raise him up and throw him over his shoulder.

" You are no weight at all, my lad," he said. " Keep still."

Little need was there for that adjuration. The wounded lad had become insensible.

Daring Dave, bracing himself for a great effort, started back at a sharp walk, which he could not maintain for more than twenty yards. The weight of his burden soon began to tell.

Every nerve was strained, his pulse throbbed fiercely, his breath came short and thick.

Then, on the verge of the wood, was heard the infuriated yells of half-a-score men of similar type to those he had already encountered.

Now was the time to drop his senseless burden and run.

But he would not do it.

" I'll save him or die !" he said, between his set teeth.

He faced round, and, gently placing the wounded sailor on the ground, prepared to fight to the last.

Alone, brave as he was, he must have fallen ; but help was at hand.

With a ringing cheer Fiery Jack, with the rest of the men, came up at a pace that caused the foe to halt suddenly and hesitate.

To hesitate is to be lost, and before the wild-eyed, swarthy ruffians could wheel about and fly, the Water-Sprites were upon them.

It was not a fight of minutes, but of moments. Down went half their number and the rest fled.

It was all over in a tenth part of the time it takes in telling.

"Well done, men !   I thank you !" cried Daring Dave.

Two of their number lifted up the wounded lad, and as they tramped back to the boat, three others, laughing and chatting meanwhile, bound up wounds they had received on the arm or shoulder.

The boat was reached, and the insensible lad laid carefully in the bows, so that his injury could be attended to as the boat went back to the ship.

The rest speedily embarked, and strong, willing arms plied the oars until there was a wide gap between the boat and the shore.

Then the foe made themselves manifest by appearing in the open from various directions.

At least a hundred came running down to the sea, brandishing knives and swords, and wasting good powder by wild, useless shots from their revolvers.

Fiery Jack and Crupper were attending to the

wounded youth, Daring Dave held the tiller-ropes, and the men pulled steadily.

There were no signs of fear or excitement, or any form of commotion.

"Them chaps is a putting theirselves into a sweat for nothing," remarked one of the oarsmen under his breath.

As he spoke the boom of one of the Water Sprite's guns was heard, and a conical shell went shrieking over their heads to the shore.

It struck the shingle with a crash, ploughed up a heap of sand and stones, and, tossing them into the air, exploded.

One of the ruffians close by was seen to be literally dashed to pieces—two others fell heavily. The rest, howling, retreated towards the wood.

"A good shot, Pegs," said Daring Dave. "Steady boys—there is no hurry."

.   .   .   .

"You see, Dave," said Jack, as he blew out a cloud of smoke from his lips, "I felt bound for once to disobey orders. I couldn't stand still and see you made mincemeat of by that gang."

"Jack, old fellow," replied Darin Dave, "you know the sort of reproof I have ready for you. I owe you my life, and I shall not forget it."

They were smoking their cigars on deck at night. Above, the stars were shining; in the west the young moon was going down.

A beautiful hour—a lovely scene—all things apparently at peace.

But there was no peace.

The dogs of war had been let loose that day. The Water Sprite was ready for immediate action.

Preparations to resist an attack upon her had been made.

The watch was fully armed, the heavy guns loaded, the men off duty sleeping with cutlass and pistol by their sides.

" The half-caste did not tell us an idle tale," said Daring Dave. " Osric Grame is no myth, and I feel sure we have dropped upon his nest. If he does not come to us to-night, to-morrow we will go to him."

CHAPTER VII.

IN SEARCH OF OSRIC GRAME—A NEW " RULE, BRITANNIA "—THE STRUGGLE IN THE HUT.

WHEN two gentlemen of the character of Aaron Nozzle and Waydown Bubbs find themselves virtually prisoners, they ought not to be surprised if great precautions are taken to retain them in custody. But these worthies, on being handcuffed on board the Water Sprite, professed the most unbounded astonishment.

Crupper, who had them under his charge, was severely cross-examined on this point ; but the only answer he gave them was—" Captain's orders, my hearties !"

They passed the night on deck, not only handcuffed but well watched over. Nothing occurred to cause any commotion on board, and at sunrise every man was astir.

The order of watches was broken up, and general breakfast was partaken of.

Daring Dave and Fiery Jack had an occasional look at the shore, but no sign of life met their view.

"The mountain won't come to Mahomet—Mahomet must go to the mountain," said the gallant captain of the Water Sprite.

His preparations were soon made.

Pegs, as usual on such occasions, was to remain in charge of the Water Sprite, with half the crew.

Dave, with the rest, were going ashore to find out, if possible, more about the piratical horde in hiding there. Fiery Jack and Crupper were to go with him in the long-boat; it would carry them all, including two men, who were to lie with it a little distance from the shore and await their return.

Rations for three days for the whole party were served out. Each man carried his cutlass, a brace of revolvers, and, in addition, had a small handy axe each, to be used, if required, in cutting down any brushwood too thick to penetrate, or for any other purpose of a like description.

The boat was lowered, the men and Crupper got into it, and Dave and Jack went below with Pegs to arrange some details of the day's work on board the Water Sprite.

Crupper was giving the men a few final hints about the use of the weapons, in which he was an admitted proficent, when he heard his name softly breathed from the deck.

Looking up he saw Vunder Fule with the inevitable trombone.

"Friend Crupper," he said, "you haf room for vun more in zat boat?"

"Two or three for the matter of that," replied Crupper, shortly; "but surely you don't think o' going?"

"It vas my tinking," answered Vunder Fule.

"See, I take my trombone to inspire you and gif de enemy more jumps."

The eye of Crupper twinkled.

"Come on," he said, "but the captain mustn't see you. Hand down that ere heavenly instrument of yours. I'll cover you both up in the bows. A few bars of that 'Winking Whale' o' yours will make them thieves as limp as dead snakes."

"I gif dem musick beans," said Vunder Fule.

They got him into the boat, and Crupper covered him up with a loose sail that was lying handy.

Two minutes afterwards Daring Dave and Fiery Jack appeared, took their seats, and the boat was headed for the shore.

In due time it grounded on the beach, when the leaders sprang out and walked slowly up the beach.

"Now's your time," said Crupper to Vunder Fule. "Out you come with us, and if the captain says anything about you being here, don't you put it on me, or I'll put a bullet through that ere trombone, lovely thing as it is."

The party hurried after Jack, and the men in charge of the boat pulled out as directed, about fifty yards from the shore. Daring Dave turned to say a few words to his men, and caught sight of Vunder Fule.

"You here ?" he exclaimed.

"Didn't you know he was coming, sir ?" said Crupper, the picture of utter amazement.

"That I certainly did not," returned Daring Dave.

"Oh ! Vunder Fule—Vunder Fule," said Crupper, shaking his hand at him ; "if you go on in this way a periverting of the truth and getting innocent people into trouble you'll come to a bad end, and your trombone too."

"I play ze martial musick," said Vunder Fule, apolegetically, " to inspire. Ze ' Dead Marsh in Saul ' —it am lovely."

The men in the boat had pulled some distance from the shore, and to hail them and send Vunder Fule back would entail a loss of time.

" It's a pity," said Daring Dave, with a vexed air ; " and you have no arms."

" I haf dis," said Vunder Fule, hoisting up the trombone.   " It gif hard knocks."

"Well, come along," said Daring Dave ; " but keep near me and do not play that—that—beas— precious trombone until I give you permission."

" Goodness send he hits somebody hard and busts it !" muttered Crupper.

Bidding his men keep well together and have their weapons ready for immediate use, Daring Dave hastened in the direction of the wood, striking it eventually at the scene of the conflict of the previous day.

There they found a very distinct trail, almost a path, by which the pirates had come and gone.

Walking with light steps, Daring Dave and Jack, with Vunder Fule, pursued their way through the wood, the men close up behind.

The trees grew thickly together and there was a considerable quantity of tangled, thorny under-growth, but nothing to bar their way.

In silence they covered fully a mile of ground, and then arrived at a spot where the trail opened into two distinct paths.

The party halted and listened for any possible sound which might serve to guide their movements, but there was not a sign of the immediate presence of a foe.

"Now, which way are we to take?" was the question asked by Fiery Jack of Daring Dave.

"Time is precious," answered Dave. "Crupper, take the men a short distance up that path—a hundred yards or so—and then return. Now, Jack, we go this way."

Vunder Fule, as he had been desired to do, kept close to his captain, and the trio walked quickly up the right-hand path.

They had traversed about fifty yards when a man leaped out of the brushwood like a startled rabbit and ran up the path.

Daring Dave called on him to stop, but he only ran the faster.

Heedless of the possibility of an ambush, Daring Dave dashed on, and his companions kept him close company. Vunder Fule, although so stout, displayed running powers of no mean order.

Suddenly, in a moment as it were, they came to the end of the wood, and before them lay an open plain.

About two hundred yards on was a big hut towards which the fugitive was hastening at the top of his speed.

He was in appearance much of the same stamp of man as the Yankees who were prisoners on board the Water Sprite. Without once looking back he raced over the ground, plunged into the hut, and closed the door.

"We must have that fellow out," said Dave.

It took very little time to cover the intervening ground, and, sword in hand, the two friends threw themselves against the door of the log hut.

It was not bolted, but somebody inside was making strenuous efforts to keep out Dave and Jack.

Vunder Fule was only a minute or two behind his leaders. The excitement of the run had inspired him with martial glory. He felt he must set his surging spirit free through the trombone or die.

"I play you battle march," he said, planting his back against the hut. "'Rule, John Bull, Britannia !'"

He was not heeded by either of the friends, who were occupied in trying to force the door, and off he went, blowing his best, and bringing something out of the trombone which might have been a chant of tortured spirits, it certainly was not "Rule, Britannia."

The door yielded a little, and Daring Dave was about to put his foot against it, when a hand, clasping a knife, was thrust out, and a blow aimed at him.

At the same moment a leery-looking ruffian, with an evil glint in his eyes, came stealing round from the back of the hut.

He had a revolver cocked ready for action.

"It seems to me," said Daring Dave, "that there are half a score fellows in this hut."

"What matters if there are a score?" said Fiery Jack. "At them, I say."

As he spoke he threw himself against the door, and, it being old and shaky, he fairly burst it off the hinges.

It fell inside, and the two plucky friends saw half-a-dozen evil faces glaring at them from the interior.

That they should hesitate before entering was

natural ; but it was only for an instant. With a cheery shout they dashed in.

At the same moment the ruffian outside came round to the front, and either not seeing Vunder Fule, or ignoring him, stepped to the doorway, and, with raised revolver, looked eagerly in.

A terrible commotion, sounds as of a fierce fight, was going on in the interior of the hut.

The fellow raised his weapon, and as he did so, the eyes of Vunder Fule fell upon him.

He stopped short in his original version of " Rule, Britannia," and with his trombone gave the ruffian a chop on the head with the edge of the big, bell-like bottom of the instrument.

Down he went to the ground, rolling about and cursing madly, as he clasped his head, which was bleeding profusely.

Having performed this feat, Vunder Fule renewed his melody.

The clashing of steel and the popping of revolvers inside the hut went on for a minute or more, and then one man, with a terrific cut from ear to chin, staggered out and fell upon the sandy soil.

He was speedily followed by two others with scared faces, who stared for a moment at Vunder Fule, and then darted away.

Again the short, sharp popping of a revolver was heard, and then the commotion suddenly ceased.

Vunder Fule stopped playing, and an expression of anxiety spread over his face.

Were the two young heroes whom he had been inspiring with martial strains *dead?*

On the ground before him lay two wounded men, writhing and groaning, inside the hut all was quiet.

But only for a little while. Soon there was a sound of moving feet, and Daring Dave, cleaned pumped out for the time being by his exertions, staggered into the open air.

Vunder Fule blew a big, terrific blast of triumph on his trombone.

"Don't," said Daring Dave, with a faint smile ; "it is too much for me now."

"Shall I play sumfin' softer ?" said Vunder Fule. "'My Mary Anne' am a good tune."

"No—no ! not yet," answered Dave. "Keep an an eye on that fellow" (pointing to the man Vunder Fule had knocked down).   "Take his arms away, and if he tries to get up shoot him. I am better now, and must see what has become of my friend."

CHAPTER VIII.

ANOTHER CAPTIVE.

EAVING Vunder Fule in charge of the wounded one we will follow Dave as he returned to the interior of the hut. It was a horrible scene he had perforce to look upon.

A few pieces of rude furniture which had been in use there were broken up almost into splinters by the fierce tramping to and fro, and, stretched upon the ground, lay five motionless men.

Four were of the foe, and the fifth was Fiery Jack.

He was bleeding from the temple, and Daring Dave leant over him and listened.

He was still breathing, but in a feeble, uncertain manner, as if his life were ebbing away.

Forgetting his own temporary weakness and all else that concerned himself Daring Dave raised his friend half up and dragged him into the open air.

With a keen, critical eye he examined the wound and an exclamation of joy escaped him.

"Only stunned!" he exclaimed. "What a narrow escape! See here, Vunder Fule, the bullet only grazed him."

"I look by-bye," said Vunder Fule, "vhen dis rascal am tied hard and fast."

Daring Dave staunched the bleeding of Jack's wound, and while in the act of binding it up with a silk handkerchief, Crupper and the men burst from the wood, and came tearing down upon the scene of the conflict.

"Why did you come alone, sir?" he said. "Goodness save us! there's been a scrimmage."

"It's over, Crupper," replied Daring Dave. "I think you had better remove those men there."

"Another Yankee, as I live!" exclaimed Crupper. "I should think the place breeds 'em like flies. Now, young man, we'll just tie your hands and legs together."

While Crupper was doing this, Jack opened his eyes, and, after a stare about him, recognised Daring Dave, and smiled.

"Quits now, I reckon," he said, "although I don't know exactly what's happened."

"You have been stunned by a random shot," replied Dave. "I have done nothing to help you."

"There you are," said Crupper, as he finished binding the captive. "What's to be done with him, cap'en?"

"Sit him up," was the reply. "I have a few questions to put to him."

Crupper sat the man up with his back to the hut, and took up a position beside him.

In this position the pair looked very much like a criminal and prison warder.

"What is your name?" asked Jack.

"Felix Carter," was the reply.

"What position do you hold with Osric Grame?"

The eyes of the man dilated with astonishment. For a brief space of time he said nothing in reply.

"What do you know of Osric Grame?" he finally enquired.

"Enough to be sure that he is a villain of the deepest dye."

"I know that and more," said Carter. "*I've* no great love for him."

"But you screen him?"

"Well, yes—much as others do—because I'm in the swim and can't get out of it."

He spoke with apparent candour, and a kinder feeling for him than he had hitherto entertained, entered the heart of Daring Dave.

"Is he here?" he said.

"On the isle—but not over handy. He's on the other side of the mountain, and there you had better leave him. The place is a regular little Gibraltar."

"Does he know I'm here?"

"I reckon not, capen. We are only an outpost here, and our orders are not to trouble the boss, unless it is for his good."

"Then he doesn't fear a foe?"

"How on earth is he to expect one?" asked Felix Carter, surprised. "Anyhow, he feels safe enough.

"Another question," said Daring Dave, "and answer me truly. We were attacked by half-breds yesterday. Who were they?"

"Most likely a hunting party. Did you lick 'em?"

"Yes."

"Oh! they won't go and tell him of that," said Carter, drily, "so you are safe there. Say, have you seen two of my mates—Aaron Nozzle and Waydown Bubbs?"

"I have them safe on board my craft," answered Daring Dave.

"Then you've got to keep an eye on 'em. They are slippery eels."

"Now, Carter, listen to me," said Dave. Have you told me the truth?"

"Nothin' but it," was the reply.

"Well, if you deceive me, you will be shot without any hesitation."

"How many men are there with Grame?"

"About two hundred—a band of all sorts—mostly no sort."

"What do you mean by that?"

"They are half-breds—mongrels—bold enough to carry out a mutiny on board a helpless ship, but not made of the true fighting stuff."

Dave glanced at Fiery Jack, who had arisen and was leaning against the hut with folded arms.

He smiled by way of reply.

Carter had conclusively confirmed the story of Wapita. It was only too true that there was such a fellow as Osric Grame, and he was entirely the villain he was reported to be.

He had also upset the little yarns spun by Nozzle and Bubbs, who might now be considered to be convicted of being part of the pirate's band.

While this examination was going on the seamen were examining the interior of the hut, where the details of the desperate conflict which had taken place were very evident.

"Bully for our capen and Fiery Jack!" said one of the men; "they are a pair of *lions*."

The dead were all swarthy men save one, and he was of the Yankee type, of the lowest order be it said. A thrust from Dave's sword had killed him.

The wounded man outside received as much care as could be given him, but he died within a quarter of an hour, and was placed inside the hut with his dead companions.

That done the door was raised up and fixed as close as possible.

Then the word was passed to return to the Water Sprite, for nothing more could be done that day.

"We must sail round the island to this new Gibraltar," said Daring Dave to Jack, "and see whether it has a soft place for us to work our way into."

"If there isn't one we'll make one, Dave."

"Well said, Jack, we will."

The legs of Felix Carter were set free so that he might walk back with the rest.

There was little danger of his getting away, as he had half the men to guard him.

He had also Vunder Fule, who looked upon him as an especial prize to watch over.

"I gif him zat open head vif ze trombone," he explained to Crupper ; " vun chop—no more."

"It seems a useful sort of harticle," replied Crupper, "as ready to knock down as to blow up. It might be turned to lots of things, too. If ever you got married you could carry the baby in it when you went out for a walk."

"No—no," sighed Vunder Fule, "I never marry. I love vonce, no more. My Gretchen marry a low fiddler."

"How long ago was that ?"

"Seven years—long years."

"And you ain't got over it yet ?"

"No, never—never. Oh ! my Gretchen. I used to play so much musick to her."

"Ah !" said Crupper, drily, "I understand the whole business now. There ain't many women who could appreciate that trombone."

"No—no," sighed Vunder Fule.

"It's kinder above 'em," muttered Crupper ; " 'tis Heavenly like. I think it's much too good for this earth."

"Vun of dese days," said Vunder Fule, gratefully, " I gif you a great treat. I gif you ' Ze Vinkle and ze Vhale' opera right trough."

"There ain't no hurry," said Crupper, with a fearful look in his eyes. " I feel that I ought to be a better man afore I'm so blessed. Music like that is much too good for a wicked man like me."

They were on their way through the wood as they talked thus together. Daring Dave called for silence. Even now a little caution was necessary.

However, no foe was at hand, and by noon the whole party was safe on board the Water Sprite.

The first thing Daring Dave did was to enquire after Sam Adams, the young sailor whom he had rescued in a wounded state on the previous day. Pegs said he was getting along amazingly.

Then he ordered Nozzle and Bubbs to be brought out and confronted with Felix Carter. Out of some possible recriminations he hoped to gain some further information about Osric Grame.

Nor was he disappointed.

When Aaron Nozzle and Waydown Bubbs were brought into the presence of Felix Carter, they saw that their little game of dissimulation was up, and, turning to Daring Dave, Aaron Nozzle said—

"Capen, we cave in and admit being no better than we should be. Isn't it so, Bubbs? Speak out, as you allus do, like a man."

"It is so," earnestly replied Bubbs.

"But what we've done we've been drove to. Ain't we, Bubbs?"

"Like sheep."

"And who drove us, but that man we see afore us."

"Him and no other."

"Hang you for a pair o' sneaking curs!" hissed Carter. "What do you mean by rounding on me? Ain't we all in the same boat?"

"I warned you times out of number," sighed Aaron Nozzle, "that your leading us into sin would get you into trouble, and you see I was right. You can't deny that."

"You camp-meeting, drivelling hypocrite!" cried Felix Carter, furiously. "If there was a specially villainous job to be done weren't you appointed to

carry it out ?   Haven't you shammed the pious seaman more than once ?"

"And I'm naturally pious," said Aaron Nozzle,
fervently, "but weak enough to be led away. Bubbs
is pious too."

Waydown Bubbs screwed his face up into what
he believed to be a saint-like expression, which
made him look more villainous than ever.

Then he and Nozzle sighed in concert, and put on
a limp attitude, with their hands clasped before
them.

"Capen," said Felix Carter to Daring Dave, "we
three are all in the pay of Osric Grame, who fully
earned the name of the Nevada Tiger before it was
given him. If you think it right to shoot or hang us
all, I freely admit that we deserve our fate, and you
won't find me drivelling when my time comes."

He had been a villain, *was* a villain still, but he
was a *man* in contrast to the others.

Dave and Jack held a short conference together,
and after it Carter was taken away and placed in
security below.   Then Crupper was called up and
received a few words of instruction.

"All right, cap'en," he said, "that's a job after
my own heart."

Meanwhile, Pegs had been busy getting up the
anchor and ordering the canvas to be set, for the
Water Sprite was going round the island to the
stronghold of the Nevada Tiger.

Crupper got a few short pieces of rope, about the
thickness of his little finger, and, having knotted
and bound them together, proceed to fix his impro-
vised cat-o'-nine-tails to the end of a short, stout
stick. Aaron Nozzle and Waydown Bubbs eyed this
proceeding with apprehension in their eyes. They

had good reason to believe that this piece of work was executed on their behalf.

They interpreted the movements of Crupper with the correctness of an infallible prophet.

" Now," said Crupper, after he had given the weapon a few experimental swishes in the air, " you two have got to walk—not run, mind you—once round the deck of this ere ship, and you are not to cut the corners off.   Most capens would have hung you right off, but we've a merciful one at the head of us, and for the present he lets you off with a larruping.   March !"

" If you touch us with that thing," said `Aaron Nozzle, "the whole of the States will rise—"

" March !"

Down came the cat-o'-nine-tails upon the back of the hypocritical ruffian, and with a howl he started on his way.

Then Waydown Bubbs received a stimulating cut, and wriggling, expostulating, whining, and roaring they staggered round the deck of the Water Sprite.

" I'll give you stripes and make you see stars," said Crupper, as he vigorously administered his blows.   " That's only in 'armony with the Yankee flag isn't it ? Stars and stripes— Slower, or I'll make you go round twice instead of once.   Stars and stripes—I don't know as ever I appreciated 'em so much afore."

Daring Dave and Fiery Jack had walked off, and stood with their backs to the scene—as if it was a matter of indifference to them ; but Pegs and the sailors enjoyed it as a rare spectacular treat.

When the round had been completed, and Nozzle and Bubbs allowed to lie down and rub themselves, a derisive cheer hailed the conclusion of the whipping entertainment.

"Two minutes for to rub the smart out, if you can," said Crupper, "and then on goes the cuffs and again you goes down into the hold to keep company with other rats, my beauties. Stars *and* Stripes ! Well, I ain't given to joking, but I think I got one in there."

CHAPTER IX.

THE STRONGHOLD OF THE NEVADA TIGER—HIS WAY OF LIVING—TREASURES OF THE DEEP.

TURN we now to the other side of the island to get a peep at the nefarious villain Osric Grame, *alias* the Nevada Tiger.

On that side of the island the mountain was almost perpendicular, being a huge cliff, with several natural terraces one under the other, ending in a wide level beach of stones and golden sands.

Advantage had been taken of these terraces to honeycomb the side of the mountain, and communication from one terrace to another was made comparatively easy by zigzag steps that had been cut in the rock.

The labour of honeycombing the mountain to a moderate depth and cutting passages and chambers in it must have been immense, but it was not the work of Osric Grame and his followers.

Ages before they saw the Many Islands some war-like race, now extinct, had made this stronghold, and of the manner of their living no record existed.

They left nothing behind them to give an inkling of their history—at least, not visible to the ordinary eye.

No stone or metal spear-heads, such as have been found in our own Devonshire caves, and elsewhere in our isles; nothing but the hollowing out of the rocks and the steps, undoubtedly the handiwork of intelligent things.

Here and there in some of the openings cannons were now placed—such pieces as were in vogue in the earlier days of our navy.

There were old-fashioned shot and powder ready to hand, and sentries were on guard night and day for a possible foe.

It is true that none had as yet appeared; but the master spirit of the band of men knew that it was wise to be always prepared, and, in addition, the discipline of men was kept up—a matter of considerable importance in such an isolated community of villainy.

The day was very young when we find the Nevada Tiger going his rounds, a duty he never neglected, to inspect his men.

Of huge build, he was fully six feet three, tall, muscular, and resolute looking, undoubtedly a man of power, and had he chosen to turn his gifts in the right direction might have been a great leader in his native land.

His attire was that of a Nevada miner, but of better materials than they can boast of, as a rule, and he carried a weapon not familiar to that class of men—a sword.

He had two attendants—one a diminutive man, who walked in a crawling manner, so that he had the appearance of being deformed.

There was craft in his face and cruelty in his eye, and the name he bore among the men was Wily Shanks.

What he lacked in skill in warfare, or anything else, he made up in cunning, and he was as dangerous as a wild cat to a foe.

The other attendant was a woman—tall, well-shaped, handsome, and graceful.

Her age was something between twenty and thirty.

Her attire was as simple as that of an Irish lass, save that she wore embroidered slippers on her feet.

Osric Grame stopped by one of the guns, where two dark-eyed, half-caste sentinels stood like statues after they had saluted him.

He cast his eye down the gun and the ammunition near, said a word or two to the men, and passed on.

Wily Shanks followed close, and the woman behind him walked with a proud step and a scornful face.

"It seems to me such mummery," she said suddenly.

"Excuse me, lady," said Wily Shanks, "but the day may come when it will be useful."

"What, so far away from the world ?"

"Lady, there is no place safe from the eyes of an English adventurer."

"Pah ! it is all mummery," the woman said.

"Lina," said Osric Grame, "peace. It is not a matter for a woman to decide."

He likewise carried a pair of the big, old-fashioned Colt revolvers in his belt.

"There is nothing here for a woman to decide," replied Lina, "but to bear her misery—like a woman."

Osric Grame was now ascending a flight of steps that led to the next terrace.

He half turned, and fixed two dark, angry eyes on her.

"Why are you ever torturing me with your impatience?" he demanded. "Yet a little while and —well, you know the rest, or shall I blab it out to all here?"

Lina muttered something, and Osric Grame went up with the hasty strides of an angry man.

On reaching the next terrace he turned to Wily Shanks, and said—

"Finish the inspection, and report to me in an hour." Then to Lina he said, curtly—

"Follow me," and plunged into an opening in the rock.

It was fully twelve feet broad and fifteen feet high, lighting a passage within for a considerable distance.

Walking along it with the haste and surefootedness of one who thoroughly knew his way, the Nevada Tiger turned to the right at the bottom, and entered a chamber of considerable dimensions, furnished in a luxurious manner.

There were chairs, tables, lounges, of the class one finds on first-class passenger ships, ornaments of various description, and even pictures.

Three oil-lamps were burning on brackets fixed upon the walls, which thoroughly illuminated the place.

The Nevada Tiger threw himself down upon a lounge, and pointed to another near him.

"Sit down," he said.

" I prefer to stand," replied the woman, coolly. "I can take your bullying much better in that position."

"Sit down, I say !"

" I mean to stand."

An impatient exclamation escaped him, and he bit his lower lip to keep back his anger.

"I ask you for the last time," he said, "not to show your teeth outside here."

" I want to go away," she replied. " You told me two years ago that I should go back to civilsation, and have the life of a princess."

" So you shall," said Osric Grame, eagerly ; " my plans are almost completed. I have wealth now such as no prince ever possessed. More than you have a knowledge of."

" Ah ! yes," she said, "treasure stained with blood. I never sleep now without being haunted with faces I have never seen ; but I know who they are. Your victims, Osric Grame."

" What madness now ?" he hissed ; " this is a new fit upon you. Turning soft, are you ?"

" So soft," she replied, with a wail, "that I wish I were at the bottom of the sea."

" It is easy enough to get there," he sneered.

"One thing stops me," said Lina, with a moan, " I dare not face death. DARE YOU ?"

He did not answer her for a moment, and his darkening brow showed how bitterly she angered him.

" Have done with this mummery," he said, finally, " or I may do something to repent of."

"Do it and *repent*," she answered.   "Shall I tell you a dream I had last night?"

"If it amuses you," he answered, drily.

"I dreamt that you sat upon a throne," said Lina, bending a little, and emphasising her utterance with graceful movements of the hand, "and around you were a host of men bowing before you, crying out, 'We humbly worship the Gold King!' Trumpets sounded, sweet singing filled the air, an intoxicating perfume was around.   You sat there in your pride."

"Well," he said, "it is a dream, and may come true."

"Hear the end," she said.   "Suddenly the circle of worshippers was parted by the coming of a fair-haired slim youth, with eyes that shot fire. All made way for him, and he walked straight up to your throne, laid a hand upon your shoulder, and, lo! all was changed.

"The crowd vanished," Lina went on, raising her voice. "The music ceased, the trumpets were still ; your throne became a heap of dead men's bones, on which you lay in the agonies of a bad man's death.   Osric Grame, there is something in my dream. Take it as a warning. Leave all here—"

"Bah!" he said, angrily, "what have I to fear?"

He paused, for hurrying footsteps were heard coming down the passage.

In a few moments Wily Shanks, panting, entered the chamber.

"What now, old fox?" cried Oscar Grame.

"Chief," almost shrieked this crouching fellow, "a strange vessel is in sight, and is bearing down upon us."

CHAPTER X.

A NAUTICAL SURVEY—LINA'S DREAM IN PART
VERIFIED—A COMPACT BETWEEN THE BEAUTY
AND THE BEAST.

SRIC GRAME leapt from the lounge and stared at the grinning Wily Shanks as if he could hardly believe his ears. Lina's eyes flashed and her nostrils dilated with excitement.

"See how soon the dream is followed by its fulfilment," she cried.

"Silence!" hissed Osric Grame. "What flag does this craft carry?"

"The English Union Jack," replied Wily Shanks.

Turning to a side-table, Osric Grame picked up a telescope lying thereon and hurried out. Wily Shanks crawled after him, and Lina, more leisurely, followed.

From the terrace Osric Grame had an extended view of the sea, and almost at his feet, as it seemed at that height, he saw the vessel which was strange to him, but is well known to the reader—viz., the Water Sprite.

The wind was soft, and she was sailing gently along, every spar and rope well defined in the clear air. On deck a few figures—mere little dolls to the watchful pirate—were moving to and fro, and in the bows a man was heaving the lead, his office proclaimed by the regularity of his movements, throwing and hauling in by turns.

"Guns—an English cruiser," said Osric Grame; "but a beggarly toy of a vessel. There is nothing to fear from her."

"She may be the pilot-fish to the shark," suggested Wily Shanks.

"Are you beginning to croak too?" demanded Osric Grame.

"Well, I don't like the look of her," replied Shanks. "She is small, but she looks as if she could bite. She is standing off now."

"Not liking the look of us," growled Osric Grame.

"There is no fear on board that vessel," said Lina. "See! they are lowering the anchor, and now they furl the canvas. Does that look like cowardice?"

Osric Grame made no reply. With his glass he was closely examining the daring little craft which had the audacity to come, in a manner of speaking, to the very door of his island home.

One of the first things he perceived was Daring Dave surveying *him* through the binoculars; and in this way two men, destined to be foes till death, first saw and took stock of each other.

"It is only some boy," said Osric Grame.

"Give me the glass," said Lina.

He handed it to her, and contemptuously turned away.

"I leave him to you," he said to Shanks; "I only fight with MEN."

"For all his boyish look," said Lina, peering through the glass, "he is a MAN—nay, more, he is the destroyer I saw in my dream."

"You lie, woman—you lie!" cried Osric Grame.

"Why should I?" she answered, coolly. "I tell you, Osric Grame, that in that vessel and its commander you have met your fate. Treat not his coming lightly."

"Pshaw! am I a woman?" demanded Osric Grame. "Enough of this prattle, Lina. Old Cunning," to Wily Shanks, "can any of the guns be brought to bear on that toy boat?"

"She is very close in," replied Shanks, "and he shows his craft by anchoring there ; but I will try."

"If the Hawk had been here," muttered Osric Grame, "she would have settled the business in an hour."

"I warned you not to let her go," said Wily Shanks. "And there is no trusting the captain. He may not think fit to return, especially if his mission is successful."

"Lacroix is true to me," said Osric Grame, "and see you that your faithfulness matches it."

"You cannot doubt me, noble chief," said Wily Shanks, crouching low.

"I trust but few," was the pirate's answer, as he re-entered the cave.

Lina was still watching the vessel below, and Wily Shanks waited until she lowered the glass before he spoke to her.

Then, creeping up to her side, he raised his eyes to hers and looked at her with a leer.

"Mistress," he said, "the chief grows less companionable to you every day."

"Indeed!" she answered, drily.

"He is tired of you, and you hate him," said Shanks. "You long to get away, but when he goes you will be left behind. Why not trust me?"

"Trust you! How?"

The crouching, cringing Shanks did not immediately reply. It evidently required a great effort for him to speak.

"Mistress," he said, "in the cave yonder there is

the chief's yacht. It is big enough for two. Say the word and I will provision her—nay, more, I can take with me jewels and gold enough to give us a life of ease. Only say the word."

"You toad! Fly with you!" said Lima, with withering disdain; "not from death itself. I have suspected that you have dared to love me."

"Mistress, can I help it?" asked Shanks, with big drops of perspiration on his brow. "Can I not see how beautiful you are? Am I not a daily witness of his treatment to you? Surely it is better to be loved by a dog than despised by a lion?"

She stood quietly listening to him, with her eyes fixed dreamily upon the sea.

He had gone too far to retreat now. A word from her to Osric Grame would lead to his death.

But would she speak it? From the sea she slowly turned her face towards him.

"I have no right to reproach you," she said, slowly. "You cannot help your form. Love is the privilege of the poorest and meanest. As for me, I am what I am. Any man has the right to speak of love to me."

She paused, and a long-drawn sigh heaved her breast. Wily Shanks cast a look back at the cavern into which Osric Grame had gone, and drew closer to her.

" Give me a word of hope," he said. " Remember, I will be lover, husband, dog, anything to you—"

"Go," she said, with sudden intensity; "obey the orders of Osric Grame, and that done, you—may—prepare the yacht!"

He would have taken her hand, but she glided away in the direction Osric Grame had taken, and left him alone.

With an exultant look upon his face he straight-ened himself up and leapt twice into the air.

Then he strode away, almost a man in his mien, muttering—

"She will go with me. She—the peerless Lina. And my life of dog to a tiger will be at an end. Lovely, sweet, charming, enchanting, entrancing Lina, the yacht shall be ready to-night."

CHAPTER XI.

THE ARRIVAL OF THE HAWK—A SHORT RUNNING FIGHT—CUTTING OUT.

"J ACK," said Daring Dave, "that place is too strong to be taken by us, except by strategy. It is, as we have been told, a small Gibraltar."

"And the beggar seems to have a lot of men under him," said Jack. "I have counted a hun-dred."

"Paraded before us to check our ardour."

"No doubt ; but that doesn't lessen the numbers. In my opinion night is the time to—"

Boom !

A gun from the shore belched out its fire, and a shot went screaming over the Water Sprite, several feet above her top hamper.

"You've judged his metal rightly, Dave," said Jack; "he can't depress his guns to hit us."

"Nor we elevate ours to do him any harm," replied Daring Dave, grimly; "and that squares matters so far. Jack, what did you think of that woman we saw up there just now?"

"Handsome enough," replied Jack, cautiously, "but a sort of tragedy queen."

"A sail!" cried Crupper, who was scanning the sea with a glass of his own—a good old-fashioned thing, about four feet long.

Dave and Jack wheeled round and saw coming round a cliff about two miles away a rakish-looking craft, low built, with tall spars, and carrying a cloud of canvas.

Of her character there could be little doubt. She was a pirate, and, as there is no need of mystery on the subject with our readers, we proclaim her to be the Hawk.

Lacroix, the captain, true to his leader, had returned from his mission, the nature of which we shall presently see.

The pirate craft was simultaneously seen from the stronghold of Osric Grame, and immediately the upper terraces were alive with men.

On came the stranger, heedless of the presence of the Water Sprite. Probably nobody on board saw her, or if they did, thought she was one of the many vessels nefariously captured and brought to the home of Osric Grame.

Daring Dave saw the position and advantage of it to himself.

He had no doubt of the real nature of the craft bearing towards him, and decided, without any preliminary proceedings, to give it a warm reception.

Swiftly the words of command fell from his lips. The sails were shaken out, and the anchor raised.

As beautiful and as graceful as a swan the Water Sprite turned her head to the sea, tacked, and bore towards the advancing vessel.

Then, with great rapidity, the outcome of good discipline and ready obedience, ammunition was brought up from below, and the guns loaded.

Meanwhile, the advancing pirate craft had been exchanging signals with the men on shore ; but apparently the full meaning of the sign of warning was not grasped, for the Water Sprite was almost within hail of the Hawk ere it was noticed.

And the next moment the character of the little craft was fully revealed by the firing of two of her guns, one shot cutting away the bowsprit, and the other hitting her aft near the water-line.

In response to this well-directed fire the pirates yelled their loudest.

There was running to and fro, and of her six visible guns three were drawn back for loading.

Swooping down upon her came the Water Sprite, firing again at two hundred yards, and receiving the return fire of the foe.

A round shot struck one of the Water Sprite men, killing him instantly, and a rope or two were cut away, and that was the extent of the injuries received.

On board the Hawk lay one of the guns, shattered and useless, and half-a-dozen groaning men.

After this fire the two vessels, being on opposite tacks, passed each other ; but, as soon as possible, the Water Sprite was brought round. The captain of the Hawk executed a similar manœuvre, and again they went at each other like two knights at a tournament.

The pirate bore towards the land, and Daring Dave had the Water Sprite steered in the same direction.

Again a broadside, such as it was, was exchanged, and the Water Sprite was struck heavily amidship. Pegs, bending over the side, saw that the hole made was low enough to take in water, and sent a man below to plug it.

" Smart's the word !" he said. " You are all wanted on deck."

The second fire of the Water Sprite had been mainly directed at the rigging of the Hawk, and chaos was made of the canvas of the mainmast. Cordage and sails came tumbling down, and hung half-way a wreck, an impediment to the further sailing of the vessel.

She was brought up as suddenly as a horse curbed with a strong hand, and swung round with her bows to the Water Sprite.

A loud hurrah burst from our gallant friends, to be instantly followed with an exclamation of dismay.

Short and sharp the Water Sprite was also brought up. She had struck on a sandbank, having, as a matter of fact, been lured into dangerous water by the cunning captain of the Hawk.

Too late Daring Dave saw that he had not tempered valour with caution.

The position of the two vessels was such that the use of their heavier metal was practically destroyed. The Water Sprite was fast aground, and the Hawk was slowly drifting away with the tide.

Daring Dave's resolves were at all times quickly taken, and never more so than on this occasion.

He ordered two of the boats to be lowered, and every available man to get into them.

"The Water Sprite must take care of herself for awhile," he said.   "She won't run away."

Half a minute sufficed to lower the boats, and a few seconds for the men to tumble into them.   The foremost to start consisted of Daring Dave and Jack and half a score men.

It was the smaller boat of the two.   The other was the long boat, and in it were Crupper, Pegs and the rest of the crew.

"Remember, lads," sang out Daring Dave, "that we've got to bring that craft back with us— and no quarter to the ruffians on board !"

"They won't give us any," muttered Crupper ; "no, not if they were paid for it."

"If a thing is paid for, sir, it isn't given," suggested one of the men.

"You keep your place," said Crupper, "and don't cut in with lopsided logic when it ain't wanted.   Derned if you won't be giving a lecture on 'stronomy next."

"Pull away, there," said Pegs ; "no talking.   If we ain't smart the cap'en will take that craft without us."

The oarsmen of both boats pulled their hardest, but the lighter craft naturally won the race.

There were fully twenty yards between them when the boat with Daring Dave overhauled the slowly drifting Hawk.

It had not been allowed to approach unmolested ; revolvers popped away merrily as they drew near, but without doing any damage, for the pirates were huddled together, impeding each other's movements, and distracting the aim of the shooters.

Daring Dave reckoned that there were at least fifty men on board. Having near thirty himself, he considered it a very even affair.

Cool, as if out on a pleasure trip, he steered the boat on to the Hawk so as to keep out of the line of fire from the big guns, and Fiery Jack fastened on with a boat-hook.

Demoniacal faces peered over the bow-side of the vessel, but a shot from Dave's revolver caused them to disappear.

Up he leaped, grasped the lower ratline, and swung himself—sword in hand—on deck.

A compact mass of ruffians was there before him.

Without looking back for his friends, he dashed in the thick of it, confident that they would not be far behind him.

Right well was his faith in them justified.

Barely had he crossed swords with the foremost when Fiery Jack was beside him, and as fast as they could follow each other his men appeared on deck.

The second boat reached the Hawk, and Crupper was the first to get over the side of the pirate craft, and found himself confronted by two swarthy ruffians, armed with the dangerous Malay creese.

"What, two to one, you lubbers!" he cried; "then here is one to two, and I hope as you've made your wills and put up your family affairs in regular order."

It is practically impossible to describe such a fight as ensued. It was a case of every man for himself, and after the first few moments there was not the least appearance of one party being arranged against another.

The deck was a scene of fragmentary warfare, if we may be allowed to use such an expression, hideous enough, in all conscience, in some of its aspects.

There was little opportunity for the use of the revolvers, but some wild shots were exchanged. The clash of steel was almost drowned in the loud yelling of the men of the Hawk.

Conspicuous in the fray was a tall, swarthy man, in picturesque attire, such as the freebooters of old used to wear. This was Lacroix, the captain of the craft, and he was the only cool man of his side.

Standing aft, he resisted the onslaught of one of the Water Sprite's men, parrying the thrusts of the cutlass, and finally wounding him.

As the man fell back he advanced a step to give him the *coup de grace*, but found a new foe ready for him in the person of Daring Dave.

Their swords crossed, and Lacroix, who smiled at first on finding himself opposed by one looking so young, very soon became grave.

He found that he had a foeman worthy of him, and if he would come off conqueror he must employ his art as a swordsman to the full.

So swiftly were the cuts and thrusts dealt and parried that the eye could not follow the movement of the weapons with accuracy, and Lacroix found himself being slowly driven back to the side of the vessel.

In vain he tried every trick and dodge with the sword he knew. Daring Dave remained unharmed, and Lacroix at last, in despair, took refuge in flight.

Swiftly turning round, he ran to the side of the vessel and leaped over into the sea.

He must have been a good diver, for although

Daring Dave watched for a few seconds he did not rise to the surface ; but, later on, he was seen making for the shore.

His ignominious flight had the inevitable effect on his men. Whatever heart they had went out of them, and, all who could, followed his example.

Many in the very act of flight were cut down, and tumbled, mortally wounded, into the sea below. Others died on the deck, snarling like wild beasts ; but a third of them succeeded in getting away.

Among the Water Sprites there were many wounds, and three of the gallants fellows, alas ! were dead.

One, a young fellow about four-and-twenty, had three pirates dead near him, no doubt slain by him ere he succumbed to numbers.

It is the lot of warfare that had laid them low, and although their messmates bewailed their loss, there was no display of outward emotion.

"Poor fellows !" said Crupper, as he helped to lay them side by side ; "they ain't half so much consarned about us as we are about them. It's a glorious death. They died like men."

As the Hawk was still drifting, and would soon be within range of the guns on shore, Daring Dave gave orders for the wrecked canvas to be cut away and cast overboard.

In half an hour it was done, and the craft, although with crippled sailing powers, was in condition to be put before the wind.

As she slowly bore up to the Water Sprite the dead pirates were consigned to the deep and the wounded attended to.

At least half-a-dozen of Daring Dave's men would be off duty for a week or so.

The dead by-and-bye would be sewn up in their hammocks, and at sunset consigned to the deep.

"It has been a severe fight," said Daring Dave to Jack, "and the cost to us has been very dear; but it is also a great victory. We have Osric Grame shut up in his den."

"It is the sort of den," replied Fiery Jack, "from which he cannot be easily dislodged.

"Well, it is worth trying," said Daring Dave; "and now let us see what is below."

CHAPTER XII.

VUNDER FULE IN SOLITUDE—THE ESCAPED PRISONER—FIRING THE WATER SPRITE, AND WHAT FOLLOWED.

AND now let us see what Vunder Fule has been doing while these stirring scenes were being enacted. He was the only person, save the three prisoners, left on board the Water Sprite, having, in fact, been forgotten. If he had been remembered, in all probability he would have been left there, for efficient as his trombone had been on one occasion, it was not exactly the weapon for continuous warfare. Sooner or later he must have suffered defeat at the hands of a better armed foe.

While the running fight was going on he was in the cuddy preparing the materials for dinner, and when the first gun was fired he certainly looked out to see what was the matter; but observing that the men were all quietly standing about the deck, he went back to his work.

"Dey haf some practice," he said. "Jiss as I haf vith my lovely child."

He patted the trombone which was in a chair near him, and proceeded to cut up some of the birds recently shot by Fiery Jack on the island, intending to make a curry.

In an undisturbed state he continued his work, not even heeding the shock of the Water Sprite going aground, and it was not until the boats had departed, and a dead silence reigned on board, that he troubled himself to look out again.

When he did so, he saw, to his amazement, that the ship was deserted.

Slowly, however, he realised the object of the boats going away, and with a satisfied smile he once more returned to his labours.

"Some more ob dem pirates," he said. "Ah! ze captain, when he settle dere hash, come back to haf curry for dinner. Hash—curry. Dat a good choke. I tell him to Mistare Cruppare when he come back."

Being short-sighted, he would not have taken in the details of the fight, and he troubled himself no more about it. Great as he was as a musician, he was a greater cook. His soul was in his work.

With great care he proceeded to concoct several delectable dishes for the captain, and at the same

time to prepare a large pot of stew for the men.
Tinned meats were brought into requisition ,and
sundry herbs which had been dried and put away.
In the matter of salt and pepper he was particular
almost to a grain.

"Good food make good digest—good digest make
ze happy man," he said.

He had been engaged thus for half an hour or
so when a slight movement on deck reached his
ears.

The cuddy door was closed to prevent the wind
blowing his herbs about, but there was a small glass
window in it which gave him a view of the deck.

Peeping through it, he saw Felix Carter standing
on deck looking cautiously about him.

On his face was an expression of surprise, which
the deserted condition of the deck amply accounted
for.

He, however, speedily grasped what was going
on, and a malevolent smile darkened his face.

An interested spectator of the attack on the pirate
vessel, he grasped the details of the fight, and as
victory gradually asserted itself on the side of the
Water Sprite, he ground his teeth and shook his
fists in impotent rage.

"Dat young man upset about sumfin," muttered
Vunder Fule. "I keep way from him now, as I
tink he gif me knocks."

One small boat remained hanging by the side of
the Water Sprite. It was the gig intended for use
when two or three men only had need to go ashore.

This Felix Carter lowered, and Vunder Fule
thought he was about to make his escape. But
that was not his immediate object.
Having lowered the gig, he went below again,

and was away about a quarter of an hour. When he appeared again on deck there was the light of malevolent joy in his eyes.

Again Vunder Fule expected he would make his way to the boat and drop down; but he had still something more to do before going away.

Advancing to the forehold, he unfastened the hatch and threw it back. As he did so the light of inspiration shone through the spectacles of Vunder Fule.

Softly opening the door, he advanced upon Felix Carter, who was in a stooping position peering into the hold.

"Hallo! you two skunks," he said.

"Is that you, Mister Carter?" asked one of the skunks, Waydown Bubbs, from below.

"Yes, it is. I have come to say good-bye."

"Are they going to let you off, Mister Carter?"

"I've let myself off. They are away, cutting out the Hawk, and I've managed to get out of my den. I hope you are pretty comfortable down there."

"No, we ain't," said Aaron Noozle. "Do help us out. Lower a rope, Mister Carter."

"What! would you take help from a wicked man who led you into evil?" chuckled Carter.

"I own I was wrong in saying that," said Aaron Nozzle; "but you'll forgive me, won't you?"

"I'm going to roast you," said Felix Carter, with sudden ferocity. "Roast you—do you hear? You are too good for this world, and in less than half an hour you'll be out of it. *I've fired the ship.*"

The two men uttered an awful howl in concert. Vunder Fule was now well on his way towards Felix Carter.

"Yes—fired the ship in the cabin next to the

spirit room," said Carter, exultingly. "I mean you to be roasted out of the world and made angels of. You good, pious folks, I—ah!"

Something butted him behind and he fell forward, his finger-tips just touching the opposite side of the opening to the hold.

He made an effort to clutch the woodwork, but missed it and went headlong down.

He fell on something soft, and as Waydown Bubbs uttered a howl and broke out into execrations immediately afterwards, it may be assumed that he was the means of saving Carter's neck as he fell.

Vunder Fule did not stay to enquire, but hurriedly put on the hatch, fastened it, and, standing up, drew a deep breath.

"I haf him," he said; "but what dat he say—ze ship on fire! *Where?*"

Seizing one of the ship's buckets, with a rope attached to it for lowering over the side, he tossed it into the sea, and drew it up full of water.

With this in his hand he hurried below as fast as his rather obese form would allow.

At the bottom of the companion he paused and sniffed. There was indeed a slight smell of fire, and a thin line of smoke was coming through the keyhole of a door on the left, opposite the captain's cabin.

Next to it was another door, where the spirits were kept, as Vunder Fule knew.

"Ah! zen I haf him," cried Vunder Fule.

He tried the door from whence smoke came. It opened to his hand, and inside he saw a mass of fire arising from piled-up wood and rubbish.

He dashed on his bucket of water, closed the door again, and returned to the deck.

Having refilled the bucket, down he went again and applied it as before. Four times did he repeat his journey ere he succeeded in getting the dangerous element under.

On the fourth visit he had sufficiently subdued it to trample out the rest.

Not until the last spark was out did he leave it and smoke-begrimed, breathless but triumphant he returned once more to the deck.

"I haf saved ze ship !" he gasped, as he leant upon one of the guns, fanning himself. "I am a brigade of fire. I put him out."

He stopped to regain his breath, and had the satisfaction of hearing a howling row in the hold. All three prisoners were yelling for help, terrified at the prospect, as even a brave man might well have been, of being burnt alive.

"It am a good fright," said Vunder Fule, complacently ; "dey haf large jomps."

The idea of his having put the fire out and the picture of the three rascals in the hold set him off chuckling until he was on the verge of choking.

A fit of coughing relieved him, and, having wiped the tears from his eyes, he went back to his cooking.

All was going on well. There was nothing for the moment to do, and he sat down to enjoy a little reflection on his recent achievement.

"I gif him push wif ze head," he said. "I butt him as ze goat, and down he go. I put out ze fire. Ah ! vat will ze capen do for me ? I ask him to let me play all ze opera of ze 'Vinkle and ze Vhale.' He says, 'Yes,' and I gif him all treats."

His eyes fell upon his loved instrument. He took it up tenderly and put the mouthpiece to his lips.

Why not now? There was nobody on board to
stop him.

He could play the whole opera through, and
nobody say a word.

But playing without an appreciative audience is
poor form to any true musician, and Vunder Fule
was about to put off the grand performance when
the thought of the three prisoners flashed upon
him.

"Zey are wicked men," he said ; "but I gif dem
treats."

Having made up his fire, and arranged his cooking utensils so that none of them would boil over,
he took a chair in one hand, and his trombone in
the other, and betook himself to the hold.

Having raised the hatch, he sat down, and checked
the appeals of the prisoners for mercy by telling
them that the fire was extinguished.

"I put him out," he said. "'I gif him vater, he
expired, and now I gif you music. De overture of
ze ' Vinkle and ze Vhale.' "

He was free to do his best or worst. The
audience was helpless, and must listen whether they
appreciated it or not.

He placed the mouthpiece to his lips, and entered
upon the most awful overture to the most horrible
opera ever written.

In two minutes the prisoners were walking about
the hold with their fingers in their ears ; in three
they were begging to be spared.

They implored, they cursed, they reviled him and
his trombone ; but he neither heard nor heeded them.

The spirit of a great musician had broken loose,
and like a flood from a reservoir it had to run its

Surely such a series of sounds have seldom been heard from an instrument—groans, shrieks, growls, rumblings. The audience forgot all other woes, and ran about the hold stopping their ears in vain.

Suddenly the noise was cut short by something being dropped over the head of Vunder Fule. His arms were pinned close to his side, and his trombone was kindly but firmly taken from him.

"You've had a festival, you have," said the voice of Crupper, as he removed his jacket with which he had enveloped the head of the great musician; "and to think of you playing to them two skunks in the hold is what I calls a heffort of genius. I hope you ain't killed 'em outright, as I think they ought to live long enough to be hung."

"Ah! friend Crupper," sighed Vunder Fule; "you cut short ze opera just as I get to ze meeting of ze vinkle and ze vhale."

"I'm sorry for the winkle," replied Crupper, "and I grieves for the whale, but I've got my orders. The capen's coming aboard directly, and he ain't got no ear for musick."

"You say of two in ze hold," said Vunder Fule, as he took back his trombone from a sailor who held it. "Dere are tree."

"Then who's third?"

"Ze gentleman of ze name of Cartare," replied Vunder Fule.

Then he told the amazed Crupper the story of the attempt to fire the ship, and how he had stifled the conflagration, and he told it in a quiet, modest manner.

"Hafing got him out," he said, "I play ze opera to rejoice."

"And, blame me!", replied Crupper, "if I ain't

sorry now I stopped you. Whether you know it or not, Mister Vunder Fule, you've done a big thing. You've saved the Water Sprite, and I, for one, should like to do something to show my gratitude. Look here, old chap! I'll tell you what I'll do. One of these days, when you and I are quite alone, far away from all other mortiful human beings, I'll let you play the rest o' that ere opera to me."

"I take your vord," said Vunder Fule, grasping his hand, "and I tank you."

"It's a bargain," said Crupper, "and I won't go back in it if it kills me. Now, here comes the captain. He's got a story to tell, too—of what he found aboard that ship. And it's a wonderful story, or I'm a sinner."

CHAPTER XIII.

VUNDER FULE PRAISED—THE IRON-BOUND BOXES —AFLOAT AGAIN.

IMMEDIATELY he arrived on board, Daring Dave, knowing Vunder Fule's peculiarities, asked why he had been performing on his trombone. The question was put good-humouredly, for Dave seemed in the highest spirits.

Vunder Fule, assisted by Crupper, explained, the great musician being very modest in his narrative.

"I do noting," he said, "but gif him push, and he go down."

"It ain't much," said Crupper, drily. "You only runned the risk of his turning round and throttling you, which he would have done in a moment, and then what would ha' come o' your trombone? Who would have been left to play it? There ain't another man in the world with half wind enough."

This is a fair specimen of how the narrative was conducted, and when Daring Dave had heard all, he said, quietly—

"Vunder Fule, you have done a great thing, and you shall not go without your reward. You have saved the Water Sprite from destruction."

Dave said nothing about the prisoners in the hold, but there was a look in his eyes which Crupper called "the dangerous twinkle," showing that they would be attended to by-and-bye.

He gave orders for the emptying of one of the store-cupboards of the Water Sprite of a great number of odds and ends.

Something that was about to be brought from the Hawk had to be put away there.

The pirate craft, in charge of Fiery Jack, was slowly beating up so as to get within easy hail of the Water Sprite.

In her crippled condition it was "creeping" rather than sailing; but time was not particularly precious.

From the shore no danger was to be apprehended. Both vessels were out of the line of fire of the pirates' guns, although many pirates were seen moving about on the bluffs ashore, eagerly watching the movements of the Hawk.

Crupper soon had the store-room ready, and shortly after the Hawk dropped anchor just outside the sand-bank on which the Water Sprite was fixed.

A number of heavily-bound iron boxes were speedily transferred from the pirate craft, and put away in the store-room

They were very heavy, and some of them required half-a-dozen men to get them below.

Vunder Fule watched this work, when he could turn his attention from his cooking, with interest. He had never before seen boxes so old or, for their size, so heavy.

"Now what do you think is in these ere things?" said Crupper, as two were being carried down—there were about a dozen in all.

"I spect—*money*," replied Vunder Fule, in a breathless whisper.

"Money, or money's worth," said Crupper. "And you've got a mind, you have, to get on it at once—but then you are bound to have no uncommon hintelect, having written such a full-blown hopera as that winkle business. The cap'en says that he's got hold of a mighty fortune, and we are all to have some of it. You'll get a tidy bit for your morning's work."

By the time the transference was done Vunder Fule had finished his cooking, and the dinner was served out, those on board the Hawk having theirs sent by the boat.

Sailors soon forget trouble and make light of sorrow, and, if for a time their dead comrades were almost forgotten, one is not disposed to condemn them.

The wounded ignored their pain, and when a man forgets his own misfortunes we cannot expect him to grieve over the loss of others.

The position of the Water Sprite was a source of anxiety; but the general opinion was that, as the bow grounded on the sand-bank at low water, she would float off with the tide.

Daring Dave and Fiery Jack were both on board watching for it.

If the high water did not lift her, it was their intention to bring the Hawk alongside, take everything movable out of her, and, by lashing her to the Water Sprite, make a raising buoy of the pirate craft. But this form of assistance was not needed.

Slowly rose the tide, and as the time for high water drew near a watchful silence fell upon all on board both vessels.

"Will she lift?" was the question in the hearts of all.

They had no fear of the gallant little vessel having suffered any material damage. She was too soundly built and had grounded too easily for any apprehension on that score.

Suddenly a faint trembling was felt. Just a little shiver—no more.

"She'll lift!" cried, or rather yelled, Crupper.

"Stand by the helm," sang out Daring Dave. "Shake out every stitch of canvas. It's a close shave," he said to Jack, who was standing by his elbow, "there is only another quarter of an hour's rising water."

Another tremble and the slightest possible tilt to leeward, the latter arising from the pressure of the wind upon the canvas. Every sail was soon set.

"She's UP!" roared Crupper, who was at the helm.

For a moment it seemed as if the Water Sprite would slowly heave over and go under water, but, having been pressed down by the breeze to a somewhat dangerous angle, her keel lifted out of the sand, she moved forward, and slowly righted

By the time she had got upon an almost even keel she had cleared the dangerous bank, and was floating safely in deep water.

A cheer rang out from those on board, and was answered by the men in charge of the Hawk.

From the shore a faint howl was borne upon the breeze. It was a cry of fury from the angry and helpless pirates.

Slowly the Water Sprite stood out, and when seven fathoms of water were reached her anchor was again dropped and her sails furled.

Meanwhile, Pegs had brought the Hawk safely round the bank, and the two vessels anchored side by side.

Strange consorts in a strange part of the world, but not destined to be long in company.

That eve, as the sun was setting, the dead seamen were reverently consigned to the deep.

In recognition of the solemnity of the time no yarn was spun that eve. Silently the watches were set, and silently passed the night.

CHAPTER XIV.

THE PLANS OF OSRIC GRAME—A DISCOVERY—A DEED OF DARKNESS.

ALL that day there had been a commotion amongst the pirates ashore. The stirring scenes at sea had been witnessed by nearly all the band, including its captain, Osric Grame.

With a bitterness that could find no adequate expression in words, he saw his craft captured by a handful of men, and its crew slain, or compelled to seek safety by swimming ashore.

About half-a-dozen, including the captain, reached the land ; the rest who leapt from the Hawk sank by the way, either from exhaustion or wounds.

Osric Grame, with the aid of his glass, saw and recognised Lacroix as he landed and, in a state of semi-exhaustion, crawled along at the base of the cliff until he reached a place which admitted of his ascending it.

Scaling it was imperative, for in a little while the rising sea would be rolling in right up to the high land.

On reaching the summit the captain of the Hawk encountered his chief, who had come out to meet him. The brow of the pirate leader was black as night.

"Lacroix," he said, "where is your manhood, to be whipped by a boy!"

"Whipped by a young fiend, with a host of raging devils behind him, you mean," replied Lacroix; "and they all bear charmed lives."

"I will see about that," said Osric Grame, "if they have the daring to land here. What a cursed misfortune! Here we are boxed up until one of my good crews bring a ship hither."

"Is there not one due?"

"Due, and overdue; but we will not talk about that just now. What of your quest?"

"I found the isle, according to the map," replied Lacroix.

"And the treasure, so long hidden from the world?"

"There, too," replied Lacroix, drily. "I brought some of it away, enough to make a man a prince of men. That has fallen into the hands of those fiends yonder."

"Was it so much?" asked Osric Grame, with an oath.

"So much, and yet but a part of the whole," answered Lacroix. "Enough remains to make others princes—kings. The hoarded treasure of great buccaneers of the past, or perchance the wealth of some forgotten monarch; but it is *there* —sixty leagues south from here, an island that rises like a desert from the sea."

"Would you had been here a day sooner, Lacroix!"

"I came with all speed, true to you."

"Lacroix, you are faithfulness itself and together

we will by-and-bye share this wealth ; but for the present we are boxed up here with no boat worthy of the name."

"And here we shall remain boxed up, unless some prize is brought in. Should it not be so, then—"

Lacroix stopped short.

The two men looked at each other with paling faces.

" If it should not be so," said Osric Grame, after a pause, "here we must remain. We have neither the means nor the men to build a boat that will take all, or a third here. Our only chance is to capture one of the vessels yonder."

" Ah ! but how ?"

" We have fifty men here who could swim out to them—you among the number !   I, alas ! could not do it. What say you, good Lacroix, to making the attempt ?"

" If you command I will obey."

" Nay, I will not command.   I will ask you as a friend. You have done too much already for me to demand more."

How oily he was—how gracious !   Lacroix was evidently pleased, for his eyes brightened and his cheek flushed.

" Chief," he said, " I will attempt it.   All I ask is food, drink, and a few hours' rest."

" Come to my own chamber and rest there," said Osric Grame.   " I will select the men who are to accompany you.   All shall be prepared.   You will —you *must*—be successful. The sleepy English-men will never dream of such an attack. They may listen for oars or the swish of advancing boats, but they will not hear the stealthy swimmer.   Go for the

Hawk. You know the way to board her. She lies low in the water."

Talking thus, the two men wended their way, first along the cliff, and then by a series of steps cut in the rock down to the cave occupied by Osric Grame.

On entering they found Lina there, lying upon a lounge, reading a book.

She just raised her eyes and then resumed her reading, taking no notice of a profound bow from Lacroix.

"Our lady is not well," whispered the captain of the Hawk.

"Pay no heed to her," growled Osric Grame; "she takes pleasure in taxing my patience. You will find wine upon the table there. Lina !"

The woman looked up again with an enquiring look—but silent.

"Get food for good Lacroix; he is hungry," said Osric Grame.

"It will be more becoming of you to wait upon him yourself," Lina answered. "I am no servant !'

"Get out of here," said Osric Grame, furiously "and do not return until I send for you."

"You will be obeyed," calmly answered Lina.

Having carefully closed the book, she rose up, and, with a quiet, majestic step, left the chamber.

"Remain here, Lacroix," said Osric Grame; "I will send you food."

He left the cave, and on the terrace outside found a servant, to whom he gave his orders, and then set out along the face of the cliff in the direction of the place where Lacroix landed.

Having got clear of his defensive works he descended to the beach, which was higher on this side, too high to be covered by the tide.

In some places there was soil deposited by occa-sional landslips, and there trees and bushes had taken root and grown apace.

This was especially the case at a spot where a waterfall had gradually cut away the cliff and created a basin of water below, from whence there was a narrow opening to the sea.

In this basin lay the small boat which Osric Grame used for pleasure trips along the coast.

It was a dapper little craft, with a cabin and sleeping accommodation for two or three persons in the form of berths at one end.

There were also cupboards in every convenient place for the storing of food, wine, and so on.

The yacht was moored in close to a landing-stage, which Osric Grame had put up.

The pirate chief had a daring project in his mind.

It was nothing more or less than to desert the island and risk alone a voyage across the sea.

First, he would visit the desert-like island and bring away as much as he could of the vast wealth which Lacroix assured him was stored there.

Then away he would go and take his chance of striking the American coast at some civilised spot.

If men have crossed the Atlantic in boats that were mere cockle-shells—and they have done so— why should he not succeed in performing the journey safely?

Anyway, it was worth trying, for the prize was freedom, wealth, and congenial society.

Stepping on board, he descended to the cabin and proceeded to examine the various boxes and lockers to see what was stored in them.

He did not expect to find much; but, to his amazement, two of them were quite full.

In one there was wine, and in the other dried fruit and meat, such as were prepared and kept stored for the use of his men.

And, what was more, these things had evidently been placed there recently.

While he was debating on this, to him, strange discovery, he heard footsteps on the landing-stage— the footsteps of a man.

Osric Grame immediately decided upon a course of action.

Pulling the curtain of one of the berths aside, he slipped in, and, quietly replacing the curtain, so as to leave himself a peeping-place, he drew one deep breath and lay still.

In a few moments Wily Shanks appeared in the cabin, bearing a big package in his arms.

Opening it, he proceeded to take out more food, wine, and cigars, which he carefully put away in one of the empty lockers, smiling and chuckling and talking to himself aloud.

What he said need not be put down here in detail. It is sufficient to say that he let his listening chief into the secret of the projected flight of himself and Lina.

What it cost the fiery chief—the Nevada Tiger—to keep quiet as he listened it is hardly possible to say, but it must have been something great in the way of effort, for when Wily Shanks at last departed and he emerged from the berth, he looked like a man who had been fighting with a powerful foe and barely escaped with life.

The perspiration was raining from his forehead, and under the brown of his skin lay a death-like, horrible whiteness, such as few could look upon without shuddering.

Opening one of the lockers, he took out a bottle of wine and, after listening to assure himself that Shanks had gone, he removed the cork by the simple process of knocking the top of the neck off with a dexterous blow with his knife.

Into a tumbler, taken out of a cupboard, he poured out some of the wine, drank it, refilled the glass, and, drinking on, finished the bottle.

"I am better now," he muttered, with a terrible smile. "They say fear kills a man. I cannot say anything about that—but I am sure rage will do it. So, my lady—you would leave me—with that wretch —that *worm!* The beautiful Lina mating with a thing that *crawls!* Ha! we shall see. Go on with your work, good Shanks—you are saving me much labour—and you shall have your reward."

The malignity expressed by his countenance was horrible.

Although he was naturally handsome, he was at that moment absolutely not human.

He would have served as a model for an artist for the figure of an agent of evil sent upon earth to ruin and destroy all that was good and beautiful.

Muttering to himself, he cleared away all signs of his presence, crept cautiously up to the deck, and went ashore.

He returned to his fortress by a circuitous route, and arrived there late in the afternoon, just as the Hawk and Water Sprite had made good their anchorage outside the sand-bank.

Having now grown calmer, he called out a number of his men, and asked for volunteers for the midnight attack upon the Hawk.

He told them that unless the vessel could be rescued they were practically imprisoned there for

any length of time, in any case as long as his foe
chose to remain near the island.

He also told them of the discovery of great wealth,
made by Lacroix, and promised the men, in case of
success, a share of it.

Finally, he declared, if they did their work well,
that their wearying life on the island should come
to an end, and that they should be taken to some
civilised place to enjoy their wealth.

Volunteers were speedily forthcoming; he
picked the men, and, bidding them assemble outside his cave a little before midnight, left them.

He was shortly after seen—gun in hand—going
up the mountain side, as he had often been seen
before, going in search of game, and none of the
men who watched his movements ever set eyes on
him again.

Then night came on, with a pleasant breeze
blowing off the shore.

The sky was cloudless and studded with stars of
surpassing brilliancy, countless in number.

At sea there was absolute silence, beyond the
slight swish of the incoming waters. On shore there
was very little movement.

Here and there a light danced about the rocks, and
there was an occasional rattle of a musket or sword
as the sentries paced to and fro—that was all.

About ten o'clock Lina passed along the face of
the rock—unchallenged by the sentries—and, descending the cliff with the sure foot of one accus-
tomed to travel in semi-darkness, hurried off in the
direction of the yacht.

She meant to fly—and had not, so far, deceived
Wily Shanks; but, in another respect, she meant
to play him false.

With woman's art she would lure him on across the sea, with false promises of being by-and-bye his wife, and, when convenient, leave him. The appointed hour for starting was to be mid-night.

There was breeze enough to take out the little yacht, a splendid sailer, going like a cork upon the sea, sailing so close to the wind at a push as to be almost in the eye of it, and, with a puff of air in its favour, indifferent to a quick, opposing tide.

Very little difficulty would there be in getting away.

Lina reached the vessel when all was dark, and, feeling her way, slipped down into the little cabin, to find two strong arms thrown around her.

"Let go, you hound!" she hissed. "I will kill you if you do not obey me."

"Nay, my love," said the voice of Osric Grame, banteringly, "is it anything new for you to have your lover's arms around you?"

Despite her resistance, he bound and gagged her in the dark, with means carefully prepared beforehand, and laid her upon the cushioned seat of the lockers.

"Lie there, my lady," he said, "until your lover comes—the sweet Wily Shanks. By my life! you are a handsome pair."

A faint moan escaped the lips of Lina, and he answered it with a mocking laugh.

"Ah! you will feel the parting from him presently," he said; "such a pretty fellow—such a charming lover."

He tightened the bandage about her mouth, until not even a groan could escape her, and then sat down in the dark to await the coming of Wily Shanks.

It was a long wait, and silence was hard to keep ; but he kept it lest he should alarm his prey.

At length the footsteps of Wily Shanks were heard upon the landing-stage, on the deck, and on the cabin stairs.

"My love," he said, softly, "are you there?"

No answer.

"Lina—pretty Lina!—don't play any tricks upon me. Everything goes well. Grame hasn't come back from his shooting, and maybe has blown his head off and rid the world of a devil. Lina, I am sure you are here. I can hear your breathing."

He came slowly into the cabin, groping his way until he was close upon Osric Grame—never more worthy of the title of Nevada Tiger than he was at that moment.

With a howl of triumphant frenzy he sprang upon the doomed Shanks, seized him by the throat, and bore him back upon the stairs.

The sound of a fierce struggle between a maddened man and a desperate one fell with appalling significance upon the ears of the helpless woman.

The horror of those few dreadful moments was something beyond the ordinary forms of earthly anguish.

Every movement, every gasp from the dying and imprecation from the living combatant were indelibly imprinted on her memory, burnt into her brain.

At last it was over, and there was a brief stillness.

Then the voice of Osric Grame was heard.

"In a few moments, my lady," he said, "I will get a light and let you look upon your lover. He will be your companion to-night while I am sailing my true little yacht across the sea."

As he spoke he struck a match, and with hands that shook lighted a swinging-lamp that hung in the middle of the cabin.

He did not look at her for some reason, probably he could not ; but, having raised up the dead man, he tossed him, an awful spectacle, down upon the seat on the opposite side of the table, and still quivering with his recent exertions, hurried out of the cabin, leaving the living and dead together.

CHAPTER XV.

A NIGHT ATTACK—THE MYSTERIOUS SHOT.

EGS, with a dozen men, had charge of the Hawk, and they had undertaken the duty of a long watch throughout the night.

There was no need to tell them to be vigilant, for, as a matter of obedience to general orders, they would be so.

Pegs posted his men round the vessel with instructions to talk very little and listen a great deal.

"Though no boat is visible," he said, "we don't know but what they've got 'em, and there's nothing like being ready for a surprise."

He spent the time walking softly about the deck

with bare feet. The night was warm, and he suffered no inconvenience, especially as he had once been an ordinary seaman, and used to that sort of thing.

It was, as he reckoned, about half an hour after midnight when a sound of something or somebody puffing, a few yards from the vessel, fell upon his ear.

Pegs at once set about seeing what it was.

With his own hands he had at an early hour fixed a rocket forward, and, running towards it, he struck a match, and applied it to the touch-paper.

Whir-r-r-r !

Aloft it went with a rush, broke with a report that was plainly heard on shore, and lighted up the ocean for a mile around.

Approaching the vessel was quite a cluster of heads—the heads of pirates advancing to attack the Hawk.

" 'Ware pirates !" he shouted.

The rocket had already created an alarm on board the Water Sprite, from whence came the sound of voices calling up those on duty.

From its deck up went another rocket.

Pegs' men were by this time all on the land side of the Hawk, ready with revolver and cutlass to repel the pirates.

"Let fly into the thick of 'em !" roared Pegs, setting the example by firing his revolver.

The popping of a dozen weapons followed, and several yells proceeded from the approaching men. High above the sounds was heard the voice of Lacroix—

"Advance ! Remember the prize before you !"

A pan of white fire was lit in the stern of the

Water Sprite, illuminating the sea. Unlike the rockets, its light did not soon die away, but burned steadily on.

Close by it stood a man keeping up the supply of the necessary material.

The pirates were taken aback, and some of them turned; but the majority, urged by Lacroix, kept steadily on.

It is not so easy to hit a man's head with a revolver as some people think, and three dozen shots from the men on the Hawk only resulted in the disappearance of four of the foe.

This was a good average, as in ordinary warfare for every man absolutely killed his weight in lead and iron is discharged from rifle and cannon.

This is a startling statement, but the statistics of material used and casualties on great battle-fields are in existence to prove it.

Pegs, by the weird light burning on the Water Sprite, saw that there was very little on that side of the Hawk to assist the foe, and, bidding the men keep cool, tightened his belt, felt the edge of his cutlass, and stood ready.

"Don't let 'em get aboard if you can help it," he said, "but if any does, *see that they go back again.*"

"Ay—ay! sir," sang out the men, cheerily.

A rattling fire was now heard from the Water Sprite, the leading sounds coming from two rifles which the men knew were handled by their young leaders.

Several heads went down one after the other, some silently, others with a terrible scream.

Foremost came Lacroix, swimming strongly and calling on his men.

Although only a pirate's tool he had pluck, and a score like him would have made tough work for Pegs and his men.

But his followers were made of more pliable stuff.

They wavered behind him, and every moment, despite his encouraging cries, one of the number turned tail and made for the shore.

When he reached the side of the Hawk he had not a score near him.

Turning to see who had kept up with him, he saw that his diminished followers would not ensure him victory ; but with a desperate cry he sprang up, grasped with one hand a chain which had escaped the lynx-eyed Pegs, and with the other drew his dripping sword.

"Follow me, men !" he cried, "and the Hawk is yours."

Pegs met him as he clambered up, and with a blow disabled his sword-arm.

But with set teeth he pulled himself over the side, slipped his sword to his left hand, and fought awhile for his life.

"Leave him to me !" cried Pegs. "Look to the others."

Pegs was an expert in the use of the cutlass, and he soon disarmed Lacroix, who, instead of giving in, flew at him like a wild cat.

"Why don't you give in, you derned fool ?" said Pegs.

"To be hanged like a dog?—never !" cried Lacroix.

"Well then, over you go," said Pegs.

Seizing the pirate by the shoulders, he twisted him round, gripped him by the waist, and carried him to the vessel's side.

Three other pirates had attempted to come on board, with the result that they had been cut down by the defenders.

A fourth was just then clambering up, and Pegs utilised Lacroix as a weapon to stop his progress.

He pitched the pirate captain clean on the top of the climbing man, and the two went down into the sea together.

This feat entirely chilled the ardour of the remainder of the band, and there was a general retreat.

After a few seconds Lacroix came up to the surface alone.

He lay upon his back swimming shoreward, and every few moments he raised his left arm, and defiantly shook his fist at his foes.

It would have been easy work to shoot him, for his progress was slow; but Pegs cried out to let him go.

"He's a blackguard, in course," he said; "but he's a brave man."

And so they let him go, with his terrified following, who had swam out in the dark for nothing.

How many reached the shore was not known; but the majority of them must have perished.

Before they had gone very far heads were seen to go down with a despairing cry, and when they were gone, and the fire on board the Water Sprite allowed to burn low, other cries came at intervals, getting fainter in turn as the defeated pirates approached the shore.

"Well done, Hawk!" sang out Daring Dave, his voice sounding clear and bell-like in the stillness of the night.

As the words left his lips the report of a rifle

rang out, and the ping of a bullet, as it struck one of the guns of the Water Sprite, was clearly heard.

Daring Dave was standing near that gun, and was uncertain as to who fired the shot.

It was startling, mysterious, and, for the instant, incomprehensible.

It could not come from one of the surviving men; for in the first place, firearms cannot be dragged through water and be of service immediately afterwards. And, in the second place, the bullet appeared to come from the sea.

" Fire a rocket !" sang out Daring Dave.

In a few moments one was soaring skyward to burst and throw its light upon the sea.

Then the mystery was explained.

Running out to sea, with a big mainsail, topsail, and jib, was a small yacht. Standing in the stern of it was Osric Grame, rifle in hand.

The light of the rocket died out, and when another was fired the little yacht was well away.

It would have been a waste of powder and shot to fire, so Daring Dave let it go. In the uncertain light he did not recognise the figure of the pirate chief, which was not to be marvelled at, as he had only seen him once through his binoculars.

" Some little sailing-vessel of the pirates," he said to Fiery Jack; "but whoever is on board can shoot. The bullet went through the lapels of my jacket, and by a little smarting near my ribs, I fancy it has grazed my skin."

The " graze," on inspection below, proved to be rather a clean cut for a bullet to make, but having put on a bandage soaked in some healing lotion, Daring Dave returned to the deck and remained on watch all night.

When the morning came the two vessels had the sea to themselves, and on the shore there were no signs of life.

The swarthy sentries had disappeared, and a close inspection of the various entrances failed to reveal a living being.

" They have cleared out," said Daring Dave.

" Or are in ambush," suggested Fiery Jack. " Suppose I go ashore to see which it is ?"

" By-and-bye," said Daring Dave ; " let the men have breakfast, and then bring up the prisoners from the hold.   With one, at least, it is folly to be any longer tender."

This was the first intimation Daring Dave had given of his intention to punish Felix Carter for his attempt to destroy the Water Sprite.

His words were caught up and passed around, to the great satisfaction of the men.

" There's no reason why we should be fooling about with that muck aboard. The Water Sprite ain't a common, low-down gaol for wagabones.   What say you, Mister Vunder Fule ?"

" If I haf de settling ob zat ting," replied Vunder Fule, " zey shall haf a short skip and a long rope, as your prophet Job say."

Breakfast was soon served out, the prisoners getting some also, which Crupper lowered to them with the comforting advice that they'd better make the most of it, as they wouldn't have many more.

Then all hands were piped for punishment, and Daring Dave took a seat on a camp-stool aft, with Fiery Jack standing beside him.

Vunder Fule was summoned to appear as a witness, and as evidence to *his* truth he brought his trombone with him.

Then Crupper, with two seamen, got the prisoners out of the hold, and marched them up to within a few feet of Dave.

They were all handcuffed now—Felix Carter sullen and defiant, Aaron Nozzle and Waydown Bubbs on the verge of tears.

Immediately they were called upon to stop the two latter fell upon their knees.

"Cap'en," said Nozzle, "have mercy on us and we'll make a clean breast o' everything."

"Stand up, if you can, like men," said Dave, sternly. "Your cowardice cannot save you."

CHAPTER XVI.

NOZZLE AND BUBBS DISMISSED—THE FATE OF CARTER—THE TRAGEDY IN THE PIRATES' STRONGHOLD.

T is necessary that we should hark back for a few hours.

Utterly and completely defeated, the pirates, or as many of them as succeeded in getting away with their lives, returned to the pirates' stronghold, there to spread about the story of the new disaster.

Lacroix was one of those who got ashore, and, humbled and crestfallen, he sought his chief to confess that the expedition had failed.

But his chief, for good reasons, he could not find. Osric Grame, as the reader knows, after performing a ghastly tragedy, had left his stronghold to take care of itself. By enquiries Lacroix learned that not only was the chief gone, but Lina and Wily Shanks also.

The conclusion that Lacroix came to was that in company they had fled, and his thoughts turned to the little yacht, in which he had had many a pleasant sail in times of leisure with Osric Grame.

Fatigued as he was with his recent futile attempt to capture the Hawk, he was, nevertheless, too impatient to wait until the morning to see if the yacht was gone, and at once went down to the little bay, where he found his worst fears verified.

"The hound—the dog!" hissed Lacroix. "He sent me on an impossible expedition that he might flee away in safety. Woe to him if ever we meet again!"

He threw himself down upon the landing-stage to think, and in a little while thought out a course of action.

As for defending the stronghold of the departed pirate-chief, that was not to be thought of. Why should he fight for the treacherous scoundrel or anything that was his?

For his own present safety and his future welfare alone would he work.

Not even the men should have the benefit of his services, for they were, as he said, " a hang-dog lot," who would be better out of the world than in it.

The plan he laid out was to take away at once certain tools, arms, ammunition, and a quantity of provisions, and do that work alone. That done, he, too, would steal away from the men, and leave them to their fate.

Of a hardy constitution and resolute disposition, the prospect of the necessary labour did not daunt him. He had several hours of darkness ahead to carry out the work—ample time. All he had to do was to procure what he needed without exciting observation.

Returning to the stronghold, he called the men together and told them that by the command of Osric Grame, who was in retirement, laying out plans for the confusion and destruction of the enemy, wine was to be served out freely, and the men were to make a merry night of it.

The store-room was a cave inside that of Osric Grame's, kept closed by a strongly built door, which was usually locked.

Lacroix had not the possession of the key, but he found a substitute in the form of an axe, and, having broken open the door, he handed out a very liberal allowance of wine, with which the gratified pirates hastened to their own quarters and proceeded to consume it.

The task of securing what he required was thus made easy, and in two hours he had carried off and hidden away in a hollow near the bay, axes, an adze, hammer, nails, and many other carpenter's tools—all, it is needless to say, the plunder from certain vessels which had fallen into the pirates' clutches.

Provisions and wine were his next care, and his last act was to deliberately spike all the big guns of the embrasures, which were, of course, in an unguarded state, the sentinels having by that time caroused themselves into a state of helpless drunkenness.

"And now, my friends," said Lacroix. grimly, " I leave you to settle the rest with the Englishmen. Au revoir !"

Returning to the Water Sprite on the morning

following the above recorded events, we take up the thread of our story at the time when Daring Dave summoned the three prisoners before him.

Aaron Nozzle and Waydown Bubbs threw themselves down upon their knees and miserably pleaded for mercy. Dave was resolved not to extend it to them—beyond giving them a bare chance of their lives.

"Loosen their bonds !" he said to Crupper, who stared at his captain in wonderment, hardly knowing if he heard aright.

"I hope you understand me, Crupper !" said Daring Dave, quietly.

Crupper, without more ado, loosened their bonds and set them free.

"Now," said Dave, "overboard you go—the pair of you !   Let us see if you can swim as well as your brother villains."

They began to vow and protest that they could not swim at all ; but Felix Carter cut them short, growling out—

"You can swim as far as that, the pair of you."

"But what sort of reception shall we get ashore ?" groaned Nozzle. "They will think we have been playing traitors to 'em."

"That is no affair of mine," rejoined Dave. "Go, and take this message with you. Within an hour I shall be ashore to try conclusions with them."

"And their answer will be a yard or two of rope for us," said Waydown Bubbs.

Dave drew out a revolver and cocked it.

"I give you both three seconds—no more—to get overboard."

"Here goes !" said Aaron Nozzle, as he ran to

the side, and, putting his hand upon the side of the vessel, "bucked" over.

Waydown Bubbs, who was by instinct and association a follower of Nozzle, immediately imitated his example.

Fiery Jack walked to the side to see what became of them.

Both dived, and were for half-a-minute under water.

Nozzle came to the surface first, and, turning over on his back, deliberately kicked off his shoes.

Waydown Bubbs, when he came to the surface, did the same, and furthermore, while treading water, pulled off his jacket.

Both were expert swimmers, and about their ability to get ashore there was very little doubt.

Meanwhile, Felix Carter was placed before Dave, who still had his revolver in his right hand, which rested on his knee. His face was very stern, and the words he uttered, though quietly spoken, fell like leaden pellets on the ear of the prisoner.

"Carter," he said, "it was my intention to have pardoned you, and perhaps taken you into my service, as soon as I found you could be trusted. Although not given your liberty, you had privileges not accorded to your fellow knaves. You requited me by making an attempt to fire my vessel."

"And would do it again if I had the chance," replied Carter, with a snarl that changed the whole appearance of his face.

Anything more horribly malignant than his expression none assembled there had ever seen.

"I made a mistake," said Dave, "as many have done before me. But I do not think I am making one now, when I sentence you to be hanged at the yard-arm—not of the Water Sprite, for I will not disgrace it with an execution, but of the Hawk. You have a quarter of an hour to live. Make the most of it."

"A quarter of an hour!" said Felix Carter, in a dull, constrained way ; "it isn't much."

"I can give you no more," replied Dave. "Crupper, I entrust you with the carrying out of my orders. If there is no volunteer executioner, let one be drawn by lot."

"I'll do it myself," replied Crupper, "and consider it nothing but my duty. Now, Mr. Black-as-night, come along."

Carter stood still, looking about him in a dull, heavy way, as if he could not quite comprehend.

The sailors had stepped back, and there were only two persons close to him, Crupper and Vunder Fule.

Into his eyes sprang a sudden fire. With one effort he burst his bonds, bowled over Crupper and Vunder Fule with a right and left blow, and rushing to the side of the vessel, sprang up like a hunted deer.

But Daring Dave had kept his eyes upon him, possibly anticipating some movement on his part.

As Felix Carter jumped, Dave raised his weapon, took rapid aim, and fired.

The bullet struck him fairly between the shoulders, cutting short his flight.

With a thud he fell upon the vessel's side, and from thence rolled into the sea. In a moment there was a dozen faces peering over to see what had become of him.

A few bubbles rose to the surface, and that was all.

A keen watch was kept around the vessel for some minutes, but he did not reappear. Felix Carter had sunk to rise no more.

"I can't help feeling sorry for him," said Dave, as he turned away with Fiery Jack, "for he had courage. But he was no more to be trusted than a tiger fresh from the jungle. What of the other two?"

"There they are, sir, getting to the shore," replied one of the men.

He pointed towards two specks, bobbing up and down upon the sea. Gradually they drew near the shore, and eventually were seen to touch the beach, and, rising up, disclose the full figures of two men.

Their after movements were watched with considerable curiosity.

First they stood still, side by side, looking up at the pirate's stronghold, where not a single man was to be seen.

Then, after apparently conferring with each other, they slowly ascended to the first terrace, and in reaching it they walked quickly into the holes or caves, and out again.

Their next move was to ascend to the second terrace, which they inspected in the same way until they came to an opening about the middle of it.

Inside this they disappeared, and were there for a considerable time.

When at length they returned to the daylight, each one carried a rifle and a bundle, with which they ran along to the end of the terrace, and disappeared.

"Now what may that mean?" asked Fiery Jack.

"It looks as if the place were deserted," replied Dave

" They've fired something inside, sir," cried
Pegs, from the deck of the Hawk; "there's the
smoke."

It was true. Out of the mouth of the cave there
came at first a thin wreath of smoke, which, however, presently increased to a volume, slowly rising
and spreading in the morning air.

A silence fell upon the watchers. Instinctively
they guessed that a dreadful crime had been committed; but how it had been made effectual they
could not tell.

But the facts were these.

Nozzle and Bubbs had gone into the chief cave,
the haunt of the ordinary pirates, and there found
the men for the most part dead drunk and all
asleep.

The appearance of the place showed that there
had been no exercise of authority for many hours.
Osric Grame, a rigid disciplinarian, could be no
longer there.

" They have killed him," said Nozzle, " and have
been making free with his wine. We can't trust
ourselves to these dark-skins. Bear a hand,
Bubbs."

In a tremor, and not daring to ask a question,
Bubbs obeyed the directions of his leader.

Half way down the cave the place narrowed and
afterwards opened out again. In shape it was
something like the old-fashioned hour-glass.

By the narrow part Nozzle, with the assistance of
Bubbs, piled up such furniture as there was—wooden
tables, chairs, and so on—with a lot of loose logs
and inflammable material under it.

A box of matches was found upon one of the men,
and after having selected a rifle for each, with

ammunition, and hastily made up a bundle of food and wine, Nozzle fired the pile.

"Clear out!" said Nozzle, "and make tracks for the middle of the island. We can hide there."

"But we shall be on the island alone," cried Bubbs.

"Isn't that better than not being alive? Come on !"

They ran on, and disappeared, as we have seen. A few minutes afterwards, the smoke came rolling out, and in a little while some living men, scorched, howling, and mad with fear.

From the deck of the two vessels they were seen to dart out of the cave—tearing off their burning clothes—frantic with pain.

Some ran blindly to the edge of the terrace, and tumbled headlong down.

Others rolled and jumped upon the ground like injured worms.

Of the majority who rushed out of the cave fully two-thirds fell heavily down, ending their agony by dashing out their brains on the rocks below.

"Whatever their crimes may have been," said Daring Dave, "they have paid a heavy penalty. But their chief has escaped."

And now came the final scene in the awful tragedy.

The men who had been rolling about in torture, got up, and, one by one, deliberately jumped from the rocky terrace, and thus in a short way put an end to their sufferings.

When the last had performed this act of despair, the pirates' haunt was a deserted fort, at the mercy of any man bold enough to step ashore and take possession.

CHAPTER XVII.

RIFLING THE PIRATES' HAUNT—THE LAST OF THE
HAWK—ON TO THE TREASURE ISLAND.

ERY rarely, if ever, has it fallen to the lot of man to make such a strange capture as that which fell into the hands of Daring Dave.

When he landed with his men the first strange sight was the dead, the fallen, crushed, and mis-shapen pirates who had escaped death by fire to blindly rush to another form of destruction.

It was a sickening, terrible sight, and he hurried up the first flight of steps, with his men at his heels, to explore the outer line of embrasures or caves in the cliffs.

No guns were there, except two or three unlimbered old ones, which had not been fired for many a day, nor was there anything in the caves to reward their search, beyond a small store of ammunition, which Dave directed to be carried to the beach in readiness to be shipped on board the Water Sprite.

The second terrace was the most important part of the stronghold.

It was longer and wider, and there were the chief armament and stores. There, also, the chief and his men once lived, for the caves, if little larger at the mouth than those below, were very deep.

Narrow passages ran from one to another, so that communication all along the line could be kept up without going outside.

In one cave were discovered several hundred-weight of powder and a goodly store of shot and shell. The latter were of little use, as they were made for a certain size of gun.

No attempt was made to carry them away, but the powder was taken down to the beach with the rest.

While the men were performing this labour Daring Dave explored the cave lately occupied by the pirate chief.

They were two in number—one for living and the other for sleeping.

In the latter the fittings were really sumptuous, and the lamp used for lighting it was of ornamented silver-work of exquisite design.

It was taken down and placed ready for removal.

The next object of great interest for Dave was a handsome writing-desk, which was unlocked.

Inside there was nothing but papers, tied up in small bundles with red tape.

The desk and its contents Dave put aside to be taken to the Water Sprite, where he could examine them at his leisure.

His next care was to collect the ornaments, most of which were of the finest workmanship, and very valuable. The furniture he had no use for, save some of the rich tapestry hangings.

There was also a big chest, unlocked and empty, which Dave suspected had recently contained valuables, which the pirate had probably carried away with him.

In the quarters of the men no search was made,

for there lay the dead, who had been smothered by the fire, the greater part of them suffocated as they slept.

Into this ghastly den Dave made no attempt to penetrate, and in no other part of the pirates' haunt was there anything worth taking away.

The third terrace was simply fitted up with guns, which, like those below, had been spiked by Lacroix, and so rendered useless.

Daring Dave found nothing of Nozzle or Bubbs, and he shrewdly guessed what had become of them.

" I could wish them no worse fate," he said, 'than to be left ashore on this island with the 'ghastly relics of a destroyed nest of villainy."

To attempt to find them would be a task embracing a length of time he could not spare, so, having removed the spoil to the Water Sprite, he returned on board.

Then his first care was to give orders for the destruction of the Hawk.

Pegs was instructed to remove it to the distance of a mile, fire it, and return to the Water Sprite.

This was a congenial task to those engaged in it, especially as the sailors had permission to remove anything they thought of value for their own benefit, providing it could be packed away without incommoding their quarters.

While these orders were being carried out Daring Dave and Jack proceeded to inspect the desk found in the cave of Osric Grame.

It contained, as we have said, nothing but papers, but in the second packet they took out they discovered something of interest.

It was a mere scrap of paper, on which was written these words—

" *The great hoard—St. Clair Island—the extreme wes isle of the Many Islands—computed at four millions— marks—a red sandstone rock, pyramid shape, and a flat sandstone, about four feet wide—dig exactly between them, four feet down, a flight of steps leading to hoarding chamber.*"

"This was written, I judge, many years ago," said Jack; "the ink is very faint."

"But it may have recently come into the possession of Osric Grame," replied Daring Dave, "and he would not in that case have had time to test the value of it."

"Perhaps he has gone to do so now," suggested Jack.

"It may be so," answered Dave. "At any rate, we will see what it is worth as soon as the Hawk is destroyed."

It was fired by this time, and they stood up to watch the black column of smoke rising from her deck. Pegs and his men were in full retreat, for they had left a certain amount of powder below to assist in the destruction of the infamous craft.

Those on board the Water Sprite watched the rapidly increasing fire, which soon reached the rigging, up which it ran swiftly, and spread the conflagration from end to end.

A quarter of an hour later the vessel blew up, and fragments were tossed round about and high into the air.

The hull, rent in twain, sank almost instantly out of sight, her disappearance being hailed by a hearty cheer from the crew of the Water Sprite.

"So perish all such blood-stained sharks of the ocean!" said Fiery Jack.

the papers, the majority of which were letters and memorandums he did not understand.

At last he came to a packet, the sight of which brought a momentary flush to his face.

It was endorsed thus—

"*The story of John Amberton's crime.   By the man who did it.*"

Fiery Jack's back was turned to him at the time, and Daring Dave, after a quick glance at his friend, put the packet into his pocket.

"It is not yet time for him to know all," he murmured.

The Water Sprite was soon at sea, under easy sail, bearing west, and a man in the bows put to watch for any change in the colour of the waves which might indicate shoaling water.

After having once got aground, Dave saw the need of extreme caution.

Ahead of them lay other islands, lying in almost a straight line to the west, the last in sight being a mere dot.

As the day was not more than half spent, they could not hope to reach the place they sought until the morn, and if the islands went further than they could see, probably not then.

But the wind being fairly on the beam, they kept on until sundown and then sought a good anchorage-ground, near a small island, about a mile long, which seemed to be entirely covered with wood.

No sign of savage or any other form of life could be seen; but, nevertheless, every precaution was taken to guard against a sudden attack from a possible foe.

No lights were to be shown, and silence on deck was commanded.

Poor Vunder Fule was, to his great grief, also docked of his usual five minutes with the trombone.

The command of Daring Dave was transmitted through Crupper, who considerately gilded the pill by saying—

" Never mind, old man ; if you wait until we can get away from these people without any ear for music, and then we'll have a go in together. You shall play and I'll sing. I never sang a song in my life, but I feel I've got one in me. I've borrowed a song-book from one of the men, and I mean to learn it right through. We'll give each other a treat, we will !"

CHAPTER XVIII.

OSCAR GRAME AND HIS VICTIM—THE TREASURE.

AIR as a dream of beauty was the morning when Osric Grame in his small yacht drew up to the Western Isle, the furthermost in that direction of the group.

It was among the smallest of them all, and had little or no verdure upon it—for it was a mass of rugged, broken, twisted rock, thrust out of the ocean by volcanic action.

But its birth was not of recent date, for it had borne the wear and tear of centuries, defying the action of time by its abounding sterility.

On other islands the birds by thousands built their homes ; but here there was no life.

It was instinctively shunned like some spot accursed.

Slowly Oscar Grame sat by the tiller, watching for some inlets into which he could guide his craft and land. In any case he would have to wade a little, but he desired to get in as close as possible.

He did not want a hiding-place, for it did not occur to him that he would be followed. No thought of the contents of the desk, or the desk itself, entered his mind.

His thoughts were entirely fixed upon two things —the treasure he sought and the woman he had in his cabin.

And as he sailed on, watching for an opening in the shore, he at the same time looked for the pyramid sandstone rock, which he knew was close to the sea.

If possible, he would like to land somewhere near it.

At last he espied it peeping above some broken ground, and his dark eyes flashed with triumph. Near it also was such a landing-place as he was seeking.

It was an opening, a mere indentation in the shore, and with a skilful hand he headed the yacht into it, lowered the mainsail, and tossed the small anchor overboard.

The sea was almost smooth, only the tiniest of waves running lazily in, to break with scarce a murmur on the rocks and sand.

To get upon dry land he had to wade through about twelve feet of shallow water.

"Lina, my queen," he said, in mocking tones, "we are at our destination. Come ashore with me, and we will rejoice over our treasure together."

There was a slight stir in the cabin, and after a short delay a soft-footed woman came slowly up into the sunlight, and stood before him.

But was *this* Lina?

Could this white-haired, aged, wild-eyed woman be the beautiful creature of two days before?

Yes; it was indeed Lina.

One night of horror unspeakable had changed her youth almost to old age.

Her hair was white as snow, and hard lines had been chiselled in her face that would never be smoothed out again until she lay still in death.

"I am here, master," she said, in a dreary tone of voice.

"It is well," was his sneering rejoinder; "it gladdens me to find you are so obedient."

She looked at him for a moment, and then turned her head away, shuddering.

"Why not end it all?" he said.

"You know I dare not," she returned; "but, oh! if you would only kill me. Be merciful and do it."

"No," he said, banteringly; "I shall take you with me so that you may see me rich and admired, a king among men. Ah! I see something in your eyes. You think that you will then betray me, but I have a weapon to use that will thwart you. I will show you as my poor sister, harmless, but mad. They will be sorry for you and pity me. Ha—ha! what sport. Come, get over and wade to the shore. I must not leave you here alone."

She obeyed him in a dull, mechanical way, wading through the water without so much as raising her dress to save it from getting wet.

He followed her, carrying a spade upon his shoulder. Together they walked to the pyramid of rock.

About twenty yards away was a big, white, flat stone.

"Sit there," he said, pointing to the left, "and watch while I unearth that which shall make me a monarch among men."

She did as she was told without a word, sitting down upon the loose stone with her hands clasped before her, the most pitiful image of misery ever seen.

If Osric Grame had owned one green spot of tenderness in his heart he would have been sorry for her; but he only laughed.

Yes, he laughed; and as he judged the spot where to strike the spade he threw his coarse badinage at her.

"You're soon tired of your lover, fair lady. But a few hours spent in staring at each other, and then at your bidding I cast him into the sea. Pah! to think of him as a man to give up all for. It was the very madness of infatuation."

"Kill me," she said, plaintively.

"No," he replied; "not for a million. Was there ever such a revenge as mine? Ask yourself if in all the history of unfaithful women one ever met with such a reward as yours?"

She bowed her head, covering her face with her hands, and he began to dig slowly, casting a glance of exultation at her from time to time.

The digging was a matter of considerable labour

for one man, and for two hours Osric Grame toiled on without stopping, save now and then to address some jeering remark to that hapless woman.

After a time she ceased to answer him, and simply sat still—a sad spectacle of dumb, hopeless misery.

At the end of two hours he rested, returning on board the yacht, accompanied by Lina—oh ! how like a cowed, well-beaten dog—to eat and drink. Afterwards he smoked at his ease, lounging in the stern of the yacht until half the afternoon was gone.

Then he resumed his labour, taking the woman ashore with him, as before, and in a short time the spade struck some hard substance beneath the sand.

With feverish haste he cleared a space disclosing a rough form of trap-door, let into a frame of rock.

By inserting the spade in the crevice between wood and stone he raised the door, disclosing a flight of steps—crudely formed by laying pieces of rock together.

" Come here, Lina !" he said, harshly ; " go down before me."

For a moment the woman hesitated.

"What are you about to do?" she asked. " Enclose me in a living tomb ?"

" Pshaw !" he said, savagely. "I simply send you first because I cannot trust you. You would like the chance of clearing out in the yacht, leaving me here to starve."

Lina rose up, and as he bade her, descended the flight of steps.

They were few in number, not more than a dozen.

At the bottom there was only a small chamber
—about six feet square—empty !

Light enough came down the opening to give a
good view of the place, and Osric Grame, standing
behind Lina, was still for awhile, staring in a dumb-
founded way at the barren rock.

"What does this mean?" he cried, hoarsely.
"Lacroix told me he had only taken a small portion
away—thinking it better to leave the greater part
for future removal.   The knave has deceived
me."

"Would any man have been in your service unless
he were a knave?"

"Keep a bridle on your tongue now," cried the
pirate, "or I may visit my disappointment on
you."

He broke out into a torrent of curses, and in a
fury struck a projecting portion of the rugged wall
with his spade.

To his astonishment the blow dislodged several
stones, which came tumbling down at his feet, disclosing an old iron-bound chest behind it.

Immediately the truth flashed upon him.

Lacroix, with the cunning of his class, had put
up a false wall to hide the treasure he left behind
him.

"Good, faithful, clever Lacroix!" cried Osric
Grame, as he dislodged one stone after another, disclosing in the end half a score chests neatly piled
one above another."

There were handles to the boxes, and, seizing one,
he dragged it out, and so heavy was the prize that
it required all his strength to perform the task.

It fell at his feet, and, the lid being unfastened, it
flew open.

Out poured a vast number of old gold coins and jewellery, set and unset.

There were bracelets, rings, chains, and loose pearls, diamonds, emeralds, rubies, and opals.

In a transport of joy Osric Grame threw himself upon the heap, dabbling in the treasure as a child plays with water.

"Mine—all mine!" he cried. "Come, Lina; these must be got on board. Hold out your dress, and let me fill it."

She obeyed, and, using his spade, he speedily filled it, and then accompanied her on board, lifting her over the side with a care he had not shown her for many a day.

The treasure trove was put away in one of the lockers, and then they returned for more. In this way two of the chests were emptied, and by that time the sun was going down.

"We will rest now," said the pirate, "until to-morrow."

He was on the yacht when he made this announcement, but Lina was still ashore, standing on a piece of rising ground and looking intently eastward.

She made no reply to Osric Grame, but continued to gaze, with her hand shading her eyes.

"What are you staring at?" impatiently asked Osric Grame.

"A sail," she replied, wheeling round and facing him. "Your Fate pursues you!"

"A lie!" yelled Osric Grame.

"Come here and see," said Lina, quietly. "It was a speck half an hour ago, and I thought little of it. Now anyone with eyes can see what it is."

The pirate sprang over the side of the vessel and waded to the shore.

With half-a-dozen bounds he was by her side, gazing eastward.

She had not lied—it was true. There was a sail, and his experienced eye told him what it was.

In a moment all things were blank before him. The principal feeling in his heart was that of fury at the prospect of being robbed of his prize.

"Fool that I was," he cried, "to fire that shot at him, otherwise he would never have known of my flight from the island."

"And even knowing so much," said Lina, "how is it that he knows you have come here?"

"How can I tell?" he snarled. "I am not good at answering conundrums. He is bearing straight upon us, but he cannot be here until dark."

"But there is to-morrow," said Lina.

"To-morrow I will be far from here," said Osric Grame. "If he has tracked us he knows nothing of the treasure. It must be hidden again."

"Can't you take it with you?"

"Do not mock me, Lina. What time have I? In two hours the tide will have ebbed away, leaving the boat aground. I shall then be a prisoner until daylight. No, we must away as soon as it is dusk. Keep by me—none of your woman's tricks."

He hastened to the hiding-place of the treasure, closed the door, and proceeded to replace the sand.

With the energy of a giant he toiled until the perspiration rained from his forehead. It was quicker work than the digging out, and half an hour after darkness had set in he had completed the task.

"It will puzzle him to guess what lies beneath here," said the pirate, as he strode towards the yacht.

" *Unless he knows,*" suggested Lina.

" How should he ?"

" There is Lacroix. His attempt to take the vessel failed. He may be a prisoner."

" He is faithful to me, and will, at least, keep silence for his own sake."

" There is one thing more," said Lina.

" What is that ?" asked Grame.

" I will tell you by-and-bye," she answered. " It is only a speculation. You have little time to get away."

" True," muttered the pirate.

In a few minutes they were on board, and Osric Grame raised the anchor, and with a spare top-mast punted the boat out of the little bay.

He was only just in time, for in going out the keel lightly touched the sand at the mouth.

In a few minutes more the passage would have been closed.

Having hoisted the sail, he bore away west, intending to go a mile or two until well clear of the island, and then to bear up on a returning tack, doubling upon his pursuers, in fact, fox fashion.

As there was no moon and he carried no light, he had no fear of being seen, and with half a breeze he would be well away out of sight ere morning.

As for the treasure, if he never secured any more of it he was rich, and if he succeeded in reaching a civilised land could live a life of ease.

He could also fit out a ship and return for the rest of his treasure trove.

These were the thoughts that passed through his mind as he stood by the helm ; close by sat Lina, still as a statue in the gloom.

"Lina," he said, suddenly, "what was the one thing more you spoke of just now?"

"The young stranger may have taken the fortress," she replied.

"What then?"

"He may have searched the place. In your desk there is a paper—"

A short, sharp exclamation of dismay escaped the pirate's lips.

It sounded especially clear in the stillness of the night, and was immediately answered by a slight commotion a short distance away.

"What was that?" asked Osric Grame, in a whisper.

"Your fate," replied Lina. "See, they haunt you. The vessel bears this way. Cannot you see her sails coming out of the darkness?"

———

CHAPTER XIX.

A CLOSE SHAVE—SAVED BY BOLDNESS—THE

GREAT PRIZE.

SRIC GRAME lost his head for a moment. The appearance of the Water Sprite was somewhat spectral in the gloom, like an avenging spirit bent upon his destruction. Like every other man he had a spirit of superstition in his nature—we all have it. It is simply a question of degree. His hand shook, and slightly relaxed its hold upon the tiller.

But the feeling of weakness departed as quickly as it came, and, confounding his childishness, he put the helm hard up, and bore away from the Water Sprite in an easterly direction.

Only just in time, for he passed within a few feet of the stern of the cruiser, so close, indeed, that he could have thrown a rope on board.

"Sail ahoy !" sang out one of the watch.

"Where away ?" cried Pegs, from amidships.

"Close astarn."

A number of rapidly given orders to bring the Water Sprite about were heard, but necessarily she had to go some distance ere the manœuvre was carried out.

Meanwhile, Osric Grame adopted a bold device.

Instead of endeavouring to sail away, he silently lowered his mainsail, and, creeping forward, took in the jib, and there was his craft riding helplessly on the ocean.

Then, addressing himself to Lina, he said, in a low, scarcely audible tone—

"Not a word—not a sound—as you value your life !"

"My life is nothing," she answered, quietly. "As for betraying you by a sound, there is no need of it. You may play the game of hide-and-seek for awhile, but you will be found out at last."

The Water Sprite was not out of sight, but in a few minutes a rocket went soaring upwards to burst and throw its weird light upon the sea.

But it was so far away that the pirate's yacht, under a bare pole, had little chance of being seen. In addition, Osric Grame reckoned those on board Daring Dave's vessel would look for a sail.

As a matter of fact they did so, and, failing to find one, they came to the conclusion that the man who gave out the warning was mistaken.

But the man was positive he had seen a square sail close under the stern of the Water Sprite, and

Pegs kept the vessel tacking about for an hour or so, sending up a rocket now and then.

But he did not tack exactly in the right direction, and each time bore further and further away from the object of his search.

It was slow work, for, being in a strange sea, in the vicinity of islands, the lead was constantly being heaved, and, finally, getting into shoaling water, the anchor was lowered and the canvas furled for the night.

Neither Dave nor Jack came on deck till afterwards, both having been taking a much needed rest.

On receiving Peg's report, they remained on deck watching with a night-glass until dawn.

Then there was nothing to be seen but the islands, the sea, and a vast quantity of gulls, the latter lightly swimming over the waves, or resting thereon, in search of food.

"The man must have been mistaken," said Jack.

"I won't be sure of that," replied Dave, "but I am troubled about our having lost sight of the pirate. I feel assured that one day I shall have him in my power. Jack, I think we have the last of the islands in sight, and this day we shall learn the value of that scrap of paper."

It was so—hard by was the westernmost island, barren, forbidding, desolate, but with soil rich with the fruit for which men toil, lie, rob, and murder—gold and jewels.

We need not linger over the search for the favoured spot. Ere noon it was found, and the Water Sprite anchored a short distance from the shore.

Dave and Jack, accompanied by Crupper and a

few sailors, landed and speedily found signs of the pirate's recent visit.

There were footmarks by the score in the sandy soil, and the track he made in going to and fro to his yacht, when it lay in the inlet, was very distinct.

" He has been here before us," said Dave, "and has, perhaps, removed the princely prize."

" Our coming may have scared him away," suggested Jack.

" True," rejoined Dave. " Measure out the distance between that rock and white stone, Crupper. Get at the exact centre, and set the men to work."

They had brought the necessary tools ashore, and the work that took Osric Grame hours to perform was done by them in a sixth of the time.

The secret cavern was soon discovered, with evidence of having been recently visited and a portion of the contents taken away, but the greater part remained.

Daring Dave made no secret of the contents of these heavy chests, of which, however, he had said not a word until they were brought to light.

And when he told them as much as there was need to tell, promising them all a share in the great discovery, a scene of wild excitement followed.

What a prospect lay ahead of them !

The voyaging of the Water Sprite over, none of them need ever work again.

To every man there would be at least a modest competency, but it was to be theirs on one condition—

Osric Grame must be captured, or his death assured of, within two years.

" You have to work, my lads," said Dave ; "and the essentials to success are vigilance, absolute obedience, and faithfulness to each other in all things. There must be no hankering after an untimely securing of the prize."

" We have taken an oath to obey you, though you end us, as a matter of duty, to certain death," said Sam Adams, advancing out of the group of seamen, " and we'll do it."

This was the young fellow who had been saved by Dave's gallantry when first they landed on the pirate's isle. He had recovered from his wounds, and was again a fine sample of the active, willing sailor, ready to do his duty, and die in the performance of it.

" I doubt none of you," said Dave, "and trust you all. This vast treasure shall be under my care until the time of distribution comes, but half of it is *yours*. And now, my lads, we will away again ; but whither I hardly know. I am like a man who gropes about in the dark for a skulking enemy ; but I am not disheartened. Within here," touching his breast, "I have a conviction that I shall find him."

The task of getting the chests on board was speedily accomplished, for all worked cheerily, and they were stowed away with the prize taken from the Hawk.

Then, with a general hilarity on board, the Water Sprite had her canvas shaken out again, and, under a light breeze, bore away eastward.

Crupper, being off duty, paid a visit to Vunder Fule, who during the scene of excitement had been calmly going on with his cooking, and told him of the wonderful discovery.

"You'll get your share of the money," said Crupper, "and will be able to treat yourself with a trombone forty feet high. You'll be able to set some music going then."

"I vant no forty feets," said Vunder Fule, "and vat you call zis a trombone for? It a Vhaleaphone, a new ting in ze vay of instruments."

"Trombone came handy," said Crupper, "and that was the name I gave it, so did t'others, and a trombone it'll be to the end of the chapter."

"It a beautiful child!" sighed Vunder Fule.

"The mystery to me," said Crupper, "is where all the sound comes from. I sometimes think you must have got some living creature inside it."

. "Der may be somefin or noting," said Vunder Fule. "I not know—I not make him."

The trombone was hanging on a nail, and Crupper, walking up to it, peered into its broad mouth.

"I can't see the bottom," he said. "But I've got it into my head that there's somebody living down there, who is quiet and happy enough until you blow into it, and then he or she—whichsumever it may be—begins to holler."

"Mistare Crupper," said Vunder Fule, "you all choke!"

"Joke!" exclaimed Crupper. "There's no joking in me. In common with the rest on board, I takes this trombone as a serious thing. We ALL think there's something alive in it. The cap'en takes his davy—which is propriate to his name—on it. As for Mister Fiery Jack, he's of a opinion that there's two livin' beings or animals, or something, down there. And you surely ain't a-going to put your judgment on the matter agin them?"

"No," replied Vunder Fule, slowly. "But I

hope it not ze trufe. I haf ze opinion up to now zat me and ze trombone make ze music togezzer."

"All you do is to supply the wind," said Crupper, "and I must say you are good at it. If you tried you could fill out the mainsail in a calm. But about this ere party, or creature, inside the trombone, I shouldn't be surprised if he didn't come out some day, tired o' the job—on strike, you know. Well, I must be off. Good-bye!"

Crupper departed, and Vunder Fule looked after him with a puzzled expression of face.

"Is it a choke?" he muttered. "Or do he tink so? If he tink so, is—"

He took down the trombone—or whalephone, or whatever it was—and looked cautiously into it.

"Ah! it so bad to see so short," he murmured— "so little vay. But shall you be zere. I haf tink dat is vunderful voice you got, my child. Ah! yes—"

He hung up the instrument again, and, backing from it, returned to his cooking.

While engaged in his work he every now and then cast an anxious glance at his pet, as if he feared to see some living thing grow out of it.

"If Mistare Crupper choke," he muttered, "I gif him choke von day. Big choke, zat he not forget!"

And then a soft groan escaped his lips. Often and often he had wondered in his slow way where all the music of the instrument came from, and now that a solution was offered him it was not so satisfactory as it might have been.

Born and bred in Germany, nursed in his infancy on tales of genii, goblins, spirits, and other uncanny creatures, it is no wonder that his superstitious nature was touched.

He thought it was *possible* that Crupper was right, and from that moment trouble and doubt about his pet instrument lay darkly on his soul.

———

CHAPTER XX.

THE SPIRIT OF THE TROMBONE—A LAST PRIZE FOR THE PIRATE—THE FIRST BLOW.

A RESTLESS night was passed by Vunder Fule.

Instead of taking his trombone to his hammock with him he left it hanging on the nail where it had been the day before.

As a rule, he slept dreamlessly, but that night he had many hideous dreams. He went through all sorts of tortuous times with his trombone, and, awaking early, hurried up to the deck and to the cuddy, into which he burst with eager haste.

"Hein! vhat is dis?" he cried, aghast.

There was the trombone, but rising out of it was a weird, wild-eyed figure—hideous to anyone, but doubly so to him, with his misty sight.

"Safe me!" he gasped, and, staggering back, would have sat down among his pots and pans but for the friendly intervention of a saving arm.

It belonged to Crupper, who rushed in to his assistance and held him up.

Outside stood two or three sailors, grinning in a very unfeeling manner. Crupper was himself the picture of keen anxiety.

"Come out into the open air !" he cried.

He dragged out Vunder Fule and fairly carried him to the side of the vessel.

"Sit here and rest a bit," he said, "then you can tell us what is the matter."

"Ze spirit in ze trombone haf come out !" gasped the great musician.

"Sperrit !" said Crupper. "Dern his impudence ! I'll go and lay it."

Leaving Vunder Fule, he ran back to the cuddy, and laid the spirit by hauling it out and looking at it with a grim smile.

To ordinary eyes it was nothing more than a big rag doll.

Holding it behind his back, he went out again, sidling up to Vunder Fule. When he got near him he quietly tossed it over the side of the vessel into the sea.

"It's all right," he said ; "I've laid it. Niver more will it have the cheek to come out again."

Vunder Fule did not answer him. He only looked at him with a dreamy, far-away look in his eyes, as if wondering whether Crupper knew anything about that spirit.

Presently he got up, walked round Crupper, felt about his back and chest. Then he returned to the cuddy and rummaged it from end to end.

Finally he took the trombone and looked into it.

"It so strange," he said ; "but I cannot belief it to be gnome or genie."

He had another good look round, and, finally, in a serious, thoughtful way, began the work of the morning.

He would not quite believe, and yet where was the figure that had scared him?

"If it Mistare Cruppare's choke," he kept on saying to himself, "I gif him choke for choke some day."

Gaily the Water Sprite sped over the seas, passing island after island until the dismantled stronghold hove in sight.

And with it there came in view something of even greater interest.

A sail.

Yes; another vessel had been brought home by a treacherous crew, the last of a long list of prizes gained by dastardly mutiny.

Daring Dave, early apprised of its appearance, soon made out what it was, and, crowding on all sail, bore down upon it.

The Water Sprite was soon espied by those on board, and the fact of her being a stranger discovered.

Whoever was in command of her was evidently in a state of doubt, for suddenly she was put on the outward tack, standing off so as to give them a wide berth.

But Daring Dave was speedily in pursuit, and the Water Sprite, with every stitch of canvas set, glided like a thing of life over the waves.

The other vessel was rapidly overhauled, and the panic on board was made apparent by the running to and fro of the crew.

"Pegs," cried Dave, "bring her up with a shot. Don't waste it, but send it into her."

It was a congenial task for Pegs, who had the bow gun loaded, sighted it himself, and fired.

Too well aimed was the shot, for it struck her fairly amidship, on the water line, tearing open the planks, and letting in a flood of water.

She was already low down, possibly with a cargo, and in a few moments showed signs of sinking. Ere the Water Sprite could get alongside she would go down.

The pirates were seen to rush to the boats ; but Pegs, after looking for his commander for permission, again had the bow gun loaded and fired.

The shot struck her higher up, sending in every direction shattered fragments of wood and splinters. A boat that was about to be lowered fell out of one of the davits, and dangled down like a toy upon a string.   Lower and lower sank the doomed craft.

"Let her be now," cried Dave. "Nothing can save her. Furl the topsails, take in a reef of the mainsail. Port the helm easy, there."

The Water Sprite lessened her speed as soon as these orders were obeyed, and, leaving room between the other vessel and the shore, got into a position to prevent the landing of any boat that might be lowered.

One was got into the water by the terrified pirates, but ten or dozen men leaped down together and upset it.

Lower and lower sank the vessel.   Cries of terror were heard to escape those on board.

About half a score still remained on deck, running to and fro.   Soon her lower ratlines were approaching the water.   She was going down fast.

The men left on board sprang into the rigging, and ran up to the lower top.

A few yards from her some half-dozen men, who had been thrown into the sea by the overturning of the boats, were swimming for their lives.

It was fully two miles to the shore, and not a man among them could accomplish the task of getting there.

The hull was under water a few minutes later, and rested in that position for a moment. Then, straight as a part of a stage scene descending to the machinery cellar below, the rigging sank slowly down.

The maddened pirates rushed up higher and higher, fighting among themselves for precedence.

Some reached the maintop, but the greater part were knocked off in the struggle into the sea.

But it was all one. Every man was doomed.

When only a few feet of the masts remained they suddenly shot out of sight, leaving the remaining men struggling in the water.

In a little while the last man went down. He was seemingly a strong swimmer, but, seeing all his comrades had sunk, he deliberately threw up his arms and followed them.

" It is all over," said Jack. " I wonder what craft it was ?"

"What does it matter ?" answered Dave. " She has ere this been booked as lost. All sail, there, and let us away from this hateful place."

———

CHAPTER XXI.

"THE RAJAH."

EADER! did you ever hear of the Island of Palmiste? Possibly not; but it exists, and is part of Britain's great possessions.

It is a big island, and extensively cultivated, with many inhabitants of various breeds.

Its home is in a stormy part of the ocean world—between the Bay of Bengal and Mexico.

It has a governor, and soldiers, and many notable men from home. There are negroes, mulattos, and half-castes of every breed under the sun.

Few men of the planter class are so rich, for the land is good and they are prosperous, although not so wealthy as they were in the old days of slavery.

The negroes worked then. They don't now, having all registered a vow to do nothing but eat melons and lie in the sun, and most religiously they keep their word.

They have been idle from the day of their emancipation to this.

About three months after the events related in

our last chapter the arrival of two strangers caused a great commotion upon the island.

One was a tall, swarthy, handsome man, who had the appearance of an Indian potentate.

The other was a strange-looking woman, young in face, but with hair as white as snow.

They were, of course, Osric Grame and Lina.

An English vessel brought them, having picked them up at sea, adrift in a small yacht.

The story that Osric Grame told was that he had been coasting about India for pleasure "with his sister," who was an "invalid," and his little craft had been carried away by adverse winds.

His yacht was brought to the island in tow, and it certainly bore out the story of his having been for weeks adrift.

There were a quantity of feathers on board, plucked from sea-fowl, which Osric Grame had shot to save himself and his "sister" from starvation.

Lina said nothing, but her silence was taken as a confirmation of the story.

Osric Grame declared his intention of settling on the island for awhile, he having "fortunately some of his jewels on board," a few of which he sold for a large sum, and bought a mansion that had recently been the property of a planter who had gone over to the majority—in other words, had died.

He furnished it with splendour, and soon began to entertain, but Lina was absent from his table.

She was rarely seen, and never spoke to anyone.

Ere long the story got about that some great loss had shattered her mind, and Osric Grame cunningly hinted that any strange stories she might tell would be the offspring of wild fancy.

"She thinks I have been a pirate," he laughingly

said, "and talks of deeds that only monsters could perpetrate. Pray do not trouble to contradict her. It only excites her to frenzy."

The people who visited him and lived around called him "The Rajah," and confessed themselves unable to pronounce his name.

The fact was, he had given one that nobody COULD pronounce, and we need not trouble our readers with it here.

One night, when he had been about a month at St. Marie, the name of the district in which he had taken up his abode, he gave a great ball.

The governor, a number of officers and planters and their wives, and many swells gathered there by the score.

A huge chamber in the mansion, given up to dancing, was crowded, and close upon the hour of midnight the mirth and revelry were at their height.

A splendid band was pouring out the sweetest of strains, bright eyes flashed, soft whisperings filled the air. There was, apparently, no marring element abroad, when suddenly a strange stillness came upon the scene.

First of all, the band had come to the end of a waltz, which accounted for some of the quietude, but not all. The dancers stood still, their whisperings ceased. Every eye was turned to the centre of the room, where stood a strange figure—Lina.

She wore her usual simple attire, save her slippers. Her well-shaped feet were bare.

Down upon her shoulders floated her white hair, so soft and silky, and so much of it—a rich display of woman's greatest treasure.

She showed no sign of being conscious of the

great company around her, but there was nothing wild about her, save in her eyes.

After a moment's dead silence a piercing, yet musical cry burst from her lips—

"Osric Grame—pirate and murderer—where are you ?"

He was in a small adjoining room, gambling with some young officers. Her voice reached him, and, tossing down the cards, he hastily rose.

"Excuse me for a moment," he said, with a quivering lip, " I fear my sister is taken ill."

He entered the ball-room and the throng parted, making a lane so that he could pass down to the middle of the room.

With hasty strides and struggling to keep his composure, he approached Lina.

"Come away," he said, gently, "this is no place for you."

"Nor for you," she answered, in a voice not loud but clear enough to penetrate every corner of the room.

"Let me take you away," he urged, stifling his fury with an effort only a strong man could make.

" I can go by myself," she said, quietly, "when I have given you warning. Your fate is on your track. He is within hail of you."

Those who stood around saw the hue of health die away under his dark skin, and marvelled.

But some said it was only natural emotion, aroused by the strange conduct of his sister.

"Your fate," cried Lina. " He of the gallant heart and strong will. You may tell all here that I am mad, but can you say the same of him ?"

He drew up to her side, and laid a hand upon her arm.

"Will you go away from here?" he said, in a low tone.

"Yes; now that I have warned you," she answered. "Hark! the clock is striking the midnight hour—dread time for all who sin. Now the spirits are abroad seeking their prey. The ghost of the man you murdered *in the dark* is stalking about outside. *I have seen it*—SEEN IT in all the ghastliness of the last moments of his life. Osric Grame, he is waiting to accompany you down to perdition."

She pushed him aside, and, utterly indifferent to the multitude of eyes fixed upon her, walked like a queen from the room.

Murmurs of sympathy for her and the dismayed Osric Grame floated around.

The pirate, with the chill drops of terror on his brow, stared about him for a moment, and then shook off the outer signs of his emotion.

"I will get a guardian for her," he said. "She is very strange, but harmless. Think no more of what you have seen, my friends, but resume your dancing. Why is the band silent? Go on there with some of your best music. Gentlemen, the supper-table waits. Good wine is ready. Forget this unhappy scene."

But the memory of that white-haired woman and her strange utterances was not to be easily shaken off. In vain the musicians played their best, and Osric Grame urged the men to drink, and the ladies to dance and be merry.

A frost—a chilling frost—had settled upon the mirth of all.

In a little time the guests began to steal away—first by twos and threes, and then in batches.

The musicians and servants stealthily retreated, and in half an hour Osric Grame was in that splendid chamber—alone !

He had done his best to keep up appearances before his guests, but he knew that all were not satisfied.

Some had gone away with a certain stiffness in their manner which showed they were beginning to doubt him.

"It was a mad freak to bring her here," he said, half aloud, "simply to prolong my revenge. Why did I not toss her overboard into the sea ?"

"Because you did not DARE," answered a soft voice near him.

He cast a hurried glance about him. He was still alone.

Whose voice was it ?

Certainly not Lina's, for, soft as it had been, it was the voice of a man.

Could it be that of the man whose life he had taken on that memorable night ?

Was it possible that his wily follower—dead and gone sure enough, or men are not dead when the breath is out of their bodies—had come back from the deep sea to haunt him ?

He rose up and walked to a window that reached to the ground. It was open, and he stepped out upon one of the walks of the garden outside.

Before him lay a magnificent scene.

St. Marie lies by the sea, and the residence of Osric Grame was the last piece of fertile land on the borders of the sandy shore.

It stood on rising ground, a charming place, rich with foliage, fruit, and flowers, with here and there a pile of picturesque rocks and half-a-dozen caves.

It was the latter which tempted Osric Grame to buy the place. They reminded him of his other island home.

From where he stood he commanded a view of his own grounds, the shore, and the sea.

High in the heavens a full moon was shining.

To the left there was a small harbour, and dotted about outside were about fifty boats and small yachts at anchor, the property of the inhabitants and the officers residing in the place.

Far away at sea, not far from the horizon, was a lone light, resting like a star on the bosom of the deep. At another time the pirate would scarce have heeded it, but now it had an irresistible fascination over him.

Despite his efforts he could not remove his eyes from it, and soon it began to swell and swell until it was a lurid light almost blinding.

Then he staggered back with a sharp cry, as it suddenly sunk down to the dimensions of a lone star again.

" A blight upon the ship that bears it," he cried. " What has it to do with me ?"

" Much," answered a voice behind him.

He knew it well, for it was Lina's, but he hesitated to turn, fearing to find that nobody was there.

But it was Lina in the flesh, and without a sound from her naked feet she drew up nearer to him.

" Much," she said again, " for it is your evil star. It is the light that is to lay bare before the world the darkness of your life."

" You hag !" he hissed. " Why do you trouble me with your lies ?"

" It is the truth," she said ; " I feel it, Osric

Grame.   There is some link between your life and
his that brings him here.   I have had dreams."

" Confound your dreams !"

" I have had dreams, I say, of a dead man lying
in a room with you standing over him, knife in
hand, and in the dead man's face I saw the features
that are his, and which I gazed upon when his ship
lay off the island yonder.   I saw you turn to leave
the room, having done your ghastly work, when he
entered and struck you down !"

" Peace, woman !   It is all idle gabble !" said
Osric Grame.

" It is not," she replied.   " I have the gift of seeing these things, which I inherit from my mother,
who was of gipsy blood.   I can read your thoughts
now."

" Read them," he said, curtly.

" You are already planning your escape from
here," she said.   " *But you cannot go !*   The first
move you make will lead to action on the part of
the men in authority here—"

" Enough, woman !"

" You shall hear me out.   I say that an attempt
to fly will lead to your being asked to give some
clearer account of yourself.   There are some who
doubt the Rajah ; and although I am accounted
mad when I call you ' Pirate,' it sets them
thinking !"

" Fiend !" he said, hoarsely, "if you value your
life anger me no further !"

" Pshaw !" she answered, contemptuously.   "You
dare not kill me here !   The disappearance of 'your
sister' would soon be marked, and you called on to
account for her.   Osric Grame, you are a fool who
has deliberately sought out a trap and walked into it !"

He knew it was true. It was clear enough to him now that she pointed it out.

He was there, and must remain there, until some good opportunity offered for him to get away.

To attempt to leave now would raise suspicions ; to slay her might lead him to the scaffold.

"You are a fiend !" he said, in a tone of concentrated, helpless passion.

"I am what you have made me," she said. "Men who sin as you have done generally forge weapons for their own destruction."

"No more of it !" he said, fiercely. "I have yet to be convinced that I have been tracked here. I'll hear no more from you to-night."

One more glance he turned seaward, and strode into the house.

"Sleep if you can !" she cried, " and wake in the morn to find that he is here."

He wheeled round in the middle of the room, and drew out a revolver from an inside pocket.

She stood close up to the window, looking at him, a fair mark to aim at. He raised the weapon and took aim, but he did not fire.

Instead of pulling the trigger he cast the revolver upon the floor, and hastened away.

She had told him truly—he dare not kill her.

CHAPTER XXII.

HOW THE WATER SPRITE CAME TO PALMISTE—A
LIFE UPON A THREAD—WOMAN'S WIT.

IT was indeed the Water Sprite that had thus arrived at the Island of Palmiste ; but what strange chance, if chance it were, had brought her there ?   A very few words will explain it.

During the months that followed the adventures of Daring Dave at the Many Islands he had cruised about here and there, and had visited America, making enquiries for a man he was seeking.   He wanted Osric Grame.

He was so fully assured that the pirate had escaped that he never once talked of abandoning the pursuit.

Fiery Jack used to marvel at this persistence, but he asked no questions, and so they went here and there, until one day, in the Bay of Bengal, they met with an English vessel lying becalmed.

Of course, the Water Sprite, which came up with the end of the dying breeze, was becalmed too, and as there was no prospect of immediate change, an exchange of visits took place between the officers of the respective vessels.

Now, it so happened, by chance or otherwise — who can tell?—that this was the same vessel which picked up Osric Grame, and the captain, who made it one of his stock stories, told Dave all about it.

Dave listened quietly, and gave out no sign of knowing the man ; but the tidings of the pirate, thus unexpectedly imparted to him, set his blood on fire.

For reasons that will be obvious, he revealed nothing, but as soon as there was a breeze steered for Palmiste. But adverse winds delayed him at times; and it was fully three weeks afterwards when he sighted the island.

It was, indeed, one of the lights of the Water Sprite which Osric Grame had seen.

She was coming slowly in at the time, seeking anchorage.

In a little while she found it, and Dave, with Jack, went below to talk over plans for the future.

"I am now about to confide in you fully, Jack," said Dave, when they had settled down and lighted their cigars. "I think you have been wondering why I have so relentlessly pursued Osric Grame?"

"Well, that's a fact," replied Jack, laughing. "Of course, if we could have fallen in with him on his island, and put an end to his game, it would be all right; but to go on a chase, something of the wild-goose order—"

"Now, Jack, don't you jump at conclusions. Do you know why I am here?"

"No."

"Osric Grame is on the island."

And then for the first time Dave told his friend the story he had heard from the captain.

He had kept it a secret for a purpose that he at once made clear.

"Jack," he said, "I told you nothing about it just then, intending to tell you everything at the proper time. The hour for confiding in you will soon arrive—to-morrow, perhaps, and in the presence of Osric Grame."

"Dave, old fellow," said Jack, "take your own good time. We each have a secret, although mine is a poor one, and in due course—if our lives are spared—the nature of them will be revealed."

"Pass me that desk, please," said Dave.

It was the small desk of the pirate, on a locker behind Jack.

He passed it over.

Dave opened it and took out the paper endorsed "The true story of John Amberton's crime. By the man who did it."

"If anything happens to deprive me of life," he said, "read this. With the aid of another paper I have written for you to read, it will tell you all."

He replaced the papers and passed back the desk ; then, opening another locker on his left, he took out a bottle of claret.

"A toast to-night," he said, "and one only."

Placing glasses upon the table, he opened the bottle and filled them with wine.

"A speedy punishment to Osric Grame," he said, raising his glass.

It was drunk—not boisterously, but in a steady business-like way—standing.

Then they resumed their seats and smoked for awhile in silence.

It was broken by footsteps outside and a knock at the door. Pegs entered.

"Any order for the morning, sir ?"

"The gig half an hour before sunrise. I am going ashore."

"Alone, sir ?"

"No. Mr. Fenton will go with me."

"Very good, sir."

Pegs had got his orders, but he did not go ; with a curious expression of face, he lingered near the door.

Dave understood him. He had a complaint to make, and hardly knew how to begin.

"What's the matter, Pegs?" he said.

"I think, sir, as a word ought to be said to Crupper."

"What about?"

"He says he's goin' to learn to play that 'ere trombone—he'll see us blowed if he don't!" said Pegs. "We've had peace through Mister Vunder Fule not blowing into it since he saw the sperrit, and Crupper ought to know better than to revive a speeches of torture."

"Perhaps he won't do it after all," suggested Jack.

"He's bent on it," said Pegs, "and he's a-writing a hopera to perform. He calls it the Sea Sarpint and the Shrimp.'"

"Well, Pegs," said Dave, "I will say a word or two to Crupper."

Pegs went away, but outside he stopped for a moment to listen. Jack and Dave were laughing, and he went away growling.

Before daylight Pegs had the boat ready, and Jack and Dave, in the cold grey light that precedes the dawn, were taken ashore.

St. Marie proper had only a few houses clustered together, and nobody was stirring there.

Dave's object in coming ashore was to quietly make a few enquiries of anyone he might meet as to the precise whereabouts of Osric Grame.

"We are too early," he said ; "let us take a stroll along the shore."

They left the houses behind them, sauntering along the lonely beach, unconsciously approaching the residence of Osric Grame.

Early as it was, the pirate was up and about, for he had not slept all night.

As soon as there was light enough he espied the

Water Sprite, and he knew that Lina had not talked idly.

But how was it the woman was able to divine such things?

Was it true that she had uncanny powers?

It seemed so, and for the first time in his life Osric Grame felt afraid of her.

But anon he saw the boat lowered, and guessed who was coming ashore.

"So early!" he said. "What a hurry he is in to bring about the end!"

Snatching up a rifle, he hastened down to the end of the grounds, and from the shadow of one of the many caves watched the movements of Dave and Jack.

Now and then he lost sight of them, but by-and-bye they came strolling towards him, and a fierce, wild hope entered his heart.

Would they come near enough for him to shoot one—or both?

He examined his rifle and cocked it. Then, crouching by a rock, just without the cave, he laid the barrel on the top, ready to take aim and shoot.

"If he will only come so far!" he muttered.

Unconsciously Daring Dave came on, talking to Jack—careless and not dreaming of danger.

There was nothing to guide him to the fact that there was a residence near, for down by the beach Nature had a strip of land all to herself, and there the trees and bushes and wild flowers formed a screen, hiding the mansion from the passer-by.

Nearer and nearer the two friends came, and as they approached Osric Grame covered them with his rifle, taking steady aim.

At last they were level with the spot where he

was in hiding, and as if they desired to give him the full opportunity of carrying out his fell purpose, they halted and looked seaward.

Osric Grame was a dead shot, and as the distance was nothing he ought to have been sure of his aim.

He WAS sure, and with a glow of unholy joy in his breast he steadily "drew a bead" on Daring Dave, aiming at his back, between the shoulders.

At that moment the life of Dave was in the hands of his foe, and another moment might have been his last but for the intervention of a woman.

Out from the cave glided Lina, and the faint rustle of her dress caused Osric Grame to start and look round.

"What evil spirit sent you here?" he asked.

"I'm often here," she replied; "I make it my home. But why pause in your work? Use your rifle, man. Fire it; but as I live *you will not hit him.*"

"You have tampered with this weapon," he hissed.

She smiled, and, passing him, sauntered on downward to the beach.

When a few paces away she turned and looked at him steadily.

"Try it on ME," she said. "It is too late for HIM."

Dave and Jack had walked on, seeing nobody, and as she spoke were passing behind a low headland of the shore. The next moment they were out of sight.

Lina followed in the same direction, and Osric Grame hesitated to call her back.

Sitting down, he laid the rifle across his knees.

and examined it to see in what way she had tampered with it. She had not interfered with it at all.

The lock was in order ; the loading in every way correct ; bullet and powder were both there.

The fury the discovery roused within him was maddening.

"Fooled by her !" he cried, "as if I were a child. Perdition seize her !"

He sprang up, looking around for her.

Heedless of the consequences, he would have shot her ; but she had disappeared.

"Fool—fool !" said Osric Grame, smiting his breast. "You had him safe—and to be gulled so easily ! At this moment he might be lying dead there. And now—"

He could say no more ; but tossing the rifle upon his shoulder, he strode back to the house.

Not only rage, but fear filled his heart.

Why had Lina followed his foes ?

To betray him, of course. What other purpose could she have ? he thought.

What could he do to save himself?

He sat down awhile pondering, his active mind busy with a dozen plans for his safety.

It was a question of a life of ease and disgrace and death. Something must be done—and that speedily. In a few hours it would be too late.

The idea came at last—a bold expedient, but the most promising of all the thoughts that came to his aid.

Why not denounce Daring Dave as an adventurer ? He had a shrewd suspicion that the captain of the Water Sprite was not the owner of an authorised cruiser. There was not exactly the rig of a government man about him.

Possibly he might be a secret buccaneer.

Anyway, to denounce him was the safest and, indeed, the only card to play, and Osric Grame decided to put it down upon the table.

If it failed to take the lead he was a lost man.

CHAPTER XXIII.

THE WARNING—AN UNWELCOME VISITOR.

SIR HERCULES CHERRYTON, the Governor of Palmiste, sat at breakfast with his lady. He ruled the island and she ruled him, and she had just given him a bit of her mind over matters, when a servant entered and respectfully waited to be addressed.

"What is it, Boulton?" asked Sir Hercules, tartly.

"The Rajah, sir. He wishes to speak to you on very important business."

Sir Hercules, in his heart, confounded the Rajah, but he looked at his wife to know what ought to be done.

"See him," she said.

Sir Hercules went out of the room, and was absent about a quarter of an hour. He came back in a state of great agitation.

"Here is a thing !" he said. "A pirate craft has

come boldly up to St. Marie, and the Cyclops away."

"She is expected to-day, is she not?" asked Lady Cherryton, serenely.

"Yes—yes, but the fellow may get away meanwhile. He has landed boldly on the island, probably to see what there is worth taking away. I must order out a troop of men and secure him."

"Finish your breakfast first."

"No—no; it must be done at once."

And out he went. A quarter of an hour later a number of the military were out scouring that part of the island in search of Daring Dave.

Let us return to him at the spot we left him in the morning.

He and Jack sauntered, as we know, round a part of the beach out of sight of Osric Grame. There they sat down to rest awhile before returning to the town.

They were conversing in an ordinary way when Jack saw a shadow near him; looking up, he and Dave beheld Lina standing a few feet from them.

"You look surprised!" she said, ere they could speak. "I am strange to you; but I know who you are and why you have come hither."

"I have seen somebody like you," replied Jack, as he and Dave rose to their feet; "but she had dark hair."

"I am the same," Lina said, with a hard laugh. "Look at it! Changed by one night of torture!" She tossed it back from her shoulder. "Enough! I will not waste your time by telling you my story. You came for Osric Grame?"

"Yes," said Dave, wonderingly. "I came to find out what he was doing."

"He was not far from here—just now," she said, "and he knows that you are ashore. Go back to your vessel for awhile."

"Why?"

"Because it will be safer or you. I feel it is so. Return here at midnight, and I will tell you what the Wolf has done to circumvent you."

"What can he do?"

"Much. Who and what are you? Have you powers from your government to take him?"

"No."

"If you say he is Osric Grame, how will you prove it?"

"I have at least one witness, and that is yourself," said Dave.

"And I cannot help you," she replied, "for they call me MAD! Go at once, I say, back to your ship. It is not cowardice, but prudence."

There was sound sense in this advice, but Dave still hesitated.

"Where is Osric Grame?" he asked.

"Here—under another name, and here he must remain," she replied. "They have some suspicion of him, and, if he attempted to fly, would arrest him."

"What shall we do, Jack?" asked Dave.

"Return," was the reply.

"Why are you so interested in me?" Dave asked Lina.

"Because you are good and brave," she answered—"brave to rashness. Be not afraid to return; you can do nothing yet, but your time will come. Go."

"I will do as you wish," said Dave.

He raised his cap and Jack his hat. She gave

them a slight yet graceful salutation in return and glided away.

"Well, Jack," said Dave, "I don't like the look of things. It seems there is to be no plain-sailing after all."

"The woman is right," replied Jack; "you can do nothing yet, and, unless I am mistaken, you would not like to answer every question put to you."

"I would answer none."

"Then would you feel inclined to show your papers?"

"I have none to show."

"Then, Dave, it won't do to stop here. Come, let us go on board and cogitate a bit."

They returned to where they had left the boat, and found it waiting for them.

Half-a-dozen niggers, woolly about the head and ragged about the body, had put in an appearance and were closely inspecting it.

Apparently they had been asking questions of the seamen in charge, and the answers had not been quite satisfactory.

"Gorry mighty!" one was saying, "you nabal officers thing big pumpkins ob yourself. What right you got to obfuslicate your carcasers in dis island?"

"What's the matter?" asked Jack.

The niggers fell back, staring at him and Dave.

"It not a goberment ship," said the previous speaker. "Where de proper buttons? Yah! git long wif you 'posters."

"May I clear 'em out, sir?" asked one of the sailors.

Dave did not answer, but Jack said, "Certainly," and the sailor jumped out of the boat.

" Clear away, the lot of you," said the sailor.

The niggers formed up in a row, and, showing a lot of the white of their eyes, awaited his coming.

Jack and the other sailors watched with interest the result of the encounter.

Suddenly the niggers all, as one man, bent their bodies down, and charged at the sailor with their heads.

It was a sudden movement, and nearly caught him by surprise.

But he was a nimble fellow, and cleared the line at a bound, dropping upon the ground as light as a feather. Wheeling round sharp, he charged in turn upon the niggers, who were still rushing on.

Raising his foot with grand effect, he kicked four of them sprawling ere the other two knew what was up.

They saw him in time, and, straightening up, darted off to a safe distance. Then they faced about and began to jeer, not the sailor, but their companions.

" Hi ! you Moses—you others—what you doing dere on de ground? What you make alligaters ob youself for ?"

The crestfallen four got up, rubbing themselves and casting malevolent glances at the sailor, who had now taken his seat in the boat.

They said nothing until it had been pushed off and the men had settled to their oars. Then they became very defiant.

" Hi ! you 'posters—what you run way for ? Who kick de poor nigger behind? Call dat fair fight? Yah ! yah ! you—you NIGGERS !"

Then they began to throw stones, but with so wild an aim that no mischief was likely to ensue.

The others came down and joined them, forgetting the insults they had hurled at their friends.

But the four had not forgotten them, and suddenly
fell upon the two, hitting out, scratching, kicking,
and biting.

Finally the whole six got into a heap upon the
sand, and were still struggling madly when the boat
reached the Water Sprite.

Daring Dave went aft and took a seat on a camp-
stool. Jack paused to watch the issue of the
fight on shore.

The six nigger combatants were interrupted in
their deadly work by a mulatto, who, with a thick
cane in his hand, arrived upon the scene.

Without any preliminary questions he began to
lay about him with no sparing hand, and the niggers
broke up like a bundle of firewood when the string
is cut.

They spread about, and were chattering at the
mulatto like magpies, when Jack was called by
Dave and went over to him.

"See that all the men have their revolvers and
plenty of cartridges," he said. "It is possible that
we may be boarded by-and-bye."

"Would you resist your own people ?"

"Not willingly, Jack, but I don't want to be
questioned too closely just yet. I must see Osric
Grame alone before I take the big move."

Vunder Fule now appeared to learn where the
captain would have the breakfast laid.

"Below," said Dave.

Vunder Fule waddled away, and went down the
companion to lay the cloth.

He had changed but little save in his face, which

out of his nose. He was hardly the Vunder Fule of old.

For months he had not blown a note on his trombone. The memory of the strange figure he had seen in it still haunted him.

He was all this time in doubt whether it was a "choke" or not.

Many a time and oft he had appealed to Crupper and been put off with evasive replies, such as " Me joke with such a beautiful thing as that ?" or " Am I the man to think of low tricks ?"

So poor, simple, superstitious Vunder Fule remained in doubt and played no more.

Breakfast was served and the two friends sat down.

It was a leisurely meal, and they lingered long over it—until the sound of strange voices on deck fell upon their ears.

They hurried up, meeting Pegs in the gangway. The face of the second mate looked white and anxious.

" An officer," he said, " from the garrison of the island."

" Very well," said Dave. " Ask him to step below."

" There's soldiers in the boat, sir."

" Let them remain there. Send the officer below."

Then he and Jack returned to the cabin to await the coming of the visitor.

———

CHAPTER XXIV.

IN A FALSE POSITION—THE COMING OF THE CRUISER — FLIGHT, AND TO DANGEROUS REFUGE.

HE officer was a young man about twenty-three. He was in the full uniform of a captain of a foot regiment, even to the sword.

On entering the cabin he bowed to Dave, who rose to receive him, and cast a quick glance around.

"I am sorry to say I am here on rather unpleasant business," he said; "it is to look at your papers."

"By what authority?" asked Dave.

"The governor of the island," was the reply.

"That is an authority I fear I cannot recognise," said Dave, calmly.

The officer looked puzzled, and just a little distressed.

"It is an authority which, on needed occasions, is prepared to assert itself," he said.

"Understand me," said Dave; "I do not despise it, but I at this moment do not owe it allegiance— I am a free agent, roaming where I will."

"With an armed vessel?"

"As you have seen."

"I shall be glad," said the officer, "if you will go ashore with me and see the governor,"

"And if I refuse ?" said Dave.

"It will be my painful duty to arrest you," was the answer.

There was a moment's pause—Daring Dave with set lips and knitted brow, the officer quiet, but troubled.

"What is the charge against me ?" asked Dave.

"Piracy on the high seas."

"Who is my accuser ?"

"That I am not able to say."

"It is a charge easily made."

"And easily refuted. Show me your authority for sailing about with a craft of this class, and you will be left in peace."

"I will show nothing," said Dave, resolutely, "and if I am attacked I will defend myself at any risk. How many men have you brought with you."

"Not sufficient to cope with your crew," replied the officer. "Personally, I shall, with your permission, return, and bear your message of defiance to the governor. On him will rest the responsibility of making a more decided move to arrest you."

"You are at liberty to go," said Dave, "and I bid you tell him that I am no pirate, but an enemy to the breed, and that I have destroyed at least one horde, save its leader, who is living at St. Marie."

"It may be so," said the officer ; "but you must first clear yourself before you can bring a charge against another."

The justice of this course, in its ordinary application, was obvious.

"Cannot you bring the man you call Rajah and myself together ?" asked Dave.

"Why ?"

"Because he is the pirate and villain, and I am his accuser."

The officer smiled and shook his head.

"What proof have you?"

"My word."

"Oh!"

"The word of my friend here—of all my crew."

"Come ashore and make your accusation."

"Will you promise that the man shall be brought before me."

"No; I cannot. It is a question for the governor to decide."

"I see," said Dave, bitterly, "I shall be obliged, against my will, to resist authority. There are some things, among them my true name, which I will not reveal until I have Osric Grame secured."

"Osric Grame!"

"Your Rajah."

"Well," said the officer, "it is needless for me to stay. I regret your decision, because it shows against you. I can hardly believe what I have heard; but, in the face of your denial, what am I to think?"

"That I am innocent," said Dave, warmly. "It is an artful move Osric Grame has taken, but it will not serve him in the end."

The officer said no more, but took his leave.

Dave politely accompanied him on deck and saw him into his boat. It had four men to row and half a-dozen soldiers armed with rifles.

Clearly it was not a force that could cope with the men of the Water Sprite.

Dave immediately ordered the anchor to be raised and sufficient canvas set to keep his vessel sailing quietly to and fro.

His intention was to stand off and on, and if any great force was sent from the shore to put out to sea.

"I do not want the blood of any honest man upon my head!" he said. "Foiled for the moment, I am still sure that my hour will come!"

But there was one danger approaching of which he knew nothing, and that was the Cyclops, hourly expected to return to St. Marie.

She was a powerful cruiser of treble the tonnage of the Water Sprite, and carrying more than double the quantity of guns and men.

Two hours later her topsails were seen above the horizon, and reported on by the watchful look-out of the Water Sprite.

The keen eye of a sailor speedily tells the nature of a vessel, and ere long Dave knew that the war-vessel was bearing down upon him.

He immediately bore away south, hoping to get off unobserved ; but ere he had gone far three guns were fired in succession from the shore, and almost immediately the Cyclops turned in pursuit of him.

The first test between the vessels was speed, and at first Dave hoped that his little craft would be able to get away.

But he soon discovered that the Cyclops was a splendid sailer, and being, furthermore, the bigger vessel, was slowly overhauling him.

Five miles, however, were between them, and it would be hours ere they came within shot of each other.

As the day advanced the wind increased, and the Water Sprite, with every possible square inch of canvas set, cut through the sea at racing speed.

ward were made secure with double bracings, and the muzzles of the lower ones were plugged to keep out the spray.

"Supposing he catches us," said Jack, as the two friends stood aft and watched the cruiser; "what will you do?"

"Fight!" replied Dave, with his teeth set.

"Her guns will soon sink us."

"Yes, Jack; but it will be better to go down to the bottom of the sea than suffer from a false charge. We cannot clear ourselves yet. Everything is against us. The possession of so much treasure on board would condemn us. How are we to account for it? Would they believe our story? No, all would be forfeited, and we condemned—that would be a great triumph for Osric Grame."

"You are right, Dave," said Jack, sadly. "Better go to the bottom than be taken. It's rather hard—but perhaps one day others may do what we failed to accomplish ourselves—put our lives in their true light before the world."

It is no shame to the men of the Water Sprite that they all viewed the approach of the Cyclops with anxiety.

It was the first time they had been in peril from FRIENDS, and their true position was as well understood by the men as by their captain.

They knew that the Water Sprite had no authority to be afloat, armed to the teeth, and that there were many things on board which would go far to condemn her.

There was some whispering among them, and the prevailing hope was that Daring Dave would, if pushed to it, fight.

"We haven't done that craft no harm," said

Crupper, "and why, in tarnation ! can't it let us alone ?"

The Water Sprite could not put out to sea, even if her captain desired it, for that would bring him nearer to the Cyclops. The one chance of escape lay in bearing round the island.

St. Marie was soon out of sight, and the coast presented the appearance of a deserted island.

No houses were to be seen, and on the sloping ground dense dark woods shut out the view of inland things.

Presently the woods changed for barren rocks, and great bluffs and headlands towered up skyward.

The shore near the sea was no longer sand, but broken rocks, and here and some distance out ugly pieces of reef peeped up from the blue waves.

It was dangerous sailing there, and all knew it.

Pegs watched from the bows, and called out when there were signs of shoaling water or rocks ahead.

At last, rounding a headland brought them into view of the most dangerous stretch of sea they had looked upon for many a day.

Far out from the shore there were signs of reefs below the sea.

The waves broke everywhere, and the heads of the rocks in view were, as Crupper remarked, "like no end of shoals of porpoises."

To enter among them was to court destruction of the Water Sprite and death to all on board.

So near the shore had Dave brought his vessel that he had no chance of wearing so as to sail away from the dangerous spot.

All he could do was to go on—to ruin, as he feared.

"Can mortal save a craft in such a sea?" he asked himself.

He did what he could, and no man could do more.

Rapidly the commands were given to shorten sail and ease off the helm a few points north.

Aloft went the men, and four-fifths of the Water Sprite's canvas disappeared as if by magic.

But still she went on, slowly but surely, as it seemed, to her doom.

And now she was fairly among the rocks, gliding in and out, obeying the helm like a thing of life, until she came to a small open space, and then Dave dropped his anchor.

"Here," he said, "we must stop and fight. At the worst we shall only meet with death. They cannot come and take us away to a dishonourable grave."

There was less wind then, and the Water Sprite rode on an even keel—broadside to the coming Cyclops, which as yet was out of sight.

Half an hour at the outside would bring her into view, and if her commander knew the water he would bring her up just outside the rocks, and, anchoring there, speedily settle the question of supremacy of the vessels.

Humanly speaking, there was no doubt about the issue. With more and heavier guns he could pound the little Water Sprite to pieces in ten minutes.

Sometimes a chance shot from a small vessel has disabled a larger one, but it was a poor thing to rely upon.

The men on board the Cyclops were good fighters, had splendid weapons, and knew how to work them.

It was a poor look-out for Daring Dave and his men.

But they did not waste their time in dreaming of coming evil. It was better employed in preparing for their defence.

The available guns were loaded, and the men took up their posts, silently awaiting the coming of the cruiser.

———

CHAPTER XXV.

WHERE IS THE CYCLOPS?—THE HIDDEN REEF—A RESCUE.

FOR half an hour they watched anxiously, but the Cyclops did not appear.

What did it mean?

Had she abandoned the pursuit, and, if so, why?

Or was she simply exercising caution, and sailing slowly in a dangerous sea?

The half-hour extended into an hour, and the cruiser did not come in sight.

Nor was there any other vessel to be seen upon the open sea.

A change came over the feelings of our friends. Anxiety turned to impatience.

"What are they doing?" asked Jack.

"Who can tell?" replied Dave. "I can only guess at one thing. Possibly the cruiser has got into trouble—she may have run upon a rock."

"Suppose she has," said Jack, reflectively; "hadn't we better go and help them?"

"Take a boat," said Dave, "and pull to the point yonder. You will soon see what has happened. But mind you do not get aground yourself."

Jack had the longboat lowered, and with Crupper and half-a-dozen men went in quest of the cruiser. The short journey between the rocks was safely accomplished, and the open water reached.

Jack steered, and Crupper was forward, watching for dangerous reefs under the sea.

Such perils as existed they escaped, and soon came to the point, round which was a view of a long stretch of sea.

An exclamation from Crupper was the first sign of something unusual having happened. The next moment Jack saw what it was.

About a mile from the shore, in apparent deep water, the bow of a vessel was sticking out of the sea.

To the bowsprit, which stood almost upright, about a dozen men were clinging.

The whole thing was apparent at a glance.

The Cyclops had run upon a hidden reef, a regular razor-back, and speedily became a total wreck.

There was no indications of any of the crew having escaped a watery grave, save those on the bowsprit, no boats going to and fro, no heads of swimming men, no life ashore.

The catastrophe had been sudden and complete.

"We must try and save these poor fellows," said Jack. "Give way, men!"

The sailors bent to their oars and pulled steadily.

Crupper continued his watchfulness, occasionally uttering some warning cry—

"Starboard a bit, sir—another razor-back!" or "Larboard a point! There's a regular steeple rock standing up ahead."

"How on earth did the Water Sprite get through such a sea without being wrecked?" Jack asked himself.

He had no time to think the matter out, ere they were near enough to get a good view of the men upon the bowsprit.

There was one in uniform, and the rest appeared to be ordinary seamen. As the boat drew near they all cheered lustily.

"Ease off a bit, sir," cried Crupper, "and bring her round—under the bowsprit. I can hook on to the anchor chains."

The man in uniform was in the prime of life, tall, and dark, with the look of a real sailor about him. The men were first-rate specimens of the British Jack Tar.

Beyond cheering they showed no emotion. Fear was entirely absent from all.

As the boat came up, the man in uniform sang out—

"Steady, men! One at a time!"

He was low down on the bowsprit, and, by ordinary right, should have been the first to drop into the boat; but he swung himself aside, and let the men go first.

One by one they came down and settled themselves in the boat, so as to preserve its balance.

They all breathed hard for awhile when they found themselves safe, and in a few, simple words, expressed their thanks.

The officer descended last, and made his way to Jack, with whom he shook hands.

"I have to thank you for my life," he said. "May I ask if you belong to the brig we have been chasing?"

"Yes," replied Jack, smiling.

"Why on earth did you run away?"

"Because you ran after us."

" I had orders from the shore to stop you, and a confounded mess I have made of it," said the officer, whom Jack guessed was the captain of the cruiser " But I don't see they can blame me. That reef is not marked on my chart of the island."

" Perhaps it has grown up since the chart was made ?" suggested Jack.

" It doesn't matter now," sighed the captain. " We ran on it going fourteen knots, and the Cyclops—poor old girl !—was fairly broken in two. In half a minute the stern went down. It was horribly sudden. I had to swim to the fore part, and it was as much as I could do to scramble up to where you found me."

" Are there no more saved ?"

" No more !" was the gloomy reply. " There was no time for anything. The water sucked everybody down like a whirlpool. Poor fellows !"

Jack was wondering what he should do with the men he had rescued—put them ashore, or take them to the Water Sprite ? The answer was given him in an unexpected manner.

" I should like to see your captain," said the officer. " Whoever or whatever he may be, I have no power to harm him now."

" I am sure you have no reason to fear him," replied Jack.

The name of the rescued commander was Fairfield, and he told Jack that the Cyclops had been his first command. It was, as he said, " deuced unlucky " to lose her.

When he saw where the Water Sprite was lying he stared with astonishment.

" You fellows must know these waters pretty well." he said

"We don't know them at all," answered Jack. "We got in them somehow, and how we are to get out again goodness only knows."

Dave was on the look-out for the boat, and when he saw the additional men in her he knew that he had guessed aright. The Cyclops was wrecked.

The boat having been got alongside he received Captain Fairfield with courtesy, and conducted him to his cabin.

The rescued sailors were taken charge of by Crupper, who got them some refeshment, and made them very comfortable.

The men were very curious about the Water Sprite, and asked many questions about her; but just then their curiosity was not entirely gratified.

"She's a gentleman's yacht," replied Crupper.

"What! with all these guns?"

"Yes, we keep 'em for firing off on birthdays. We've a kind captain, who likes the birthday of every man to be kept."

"That be blowed for a tale!"

"Well," said Crupper, "if you don't like to believe it you needn't. You'll know by-and-bye if it's true or not."

Dave and Captain Fairfield were in close conversation for more than an hour in the cabin ere Jack, who had remained on deck, was sent for.

On entering the cabin he was greeted warmly by the late commander of the Cyclops.

"Sufficient has been told me," he said, "for me to know that the people ashore have acted like fools. They have been gulled by a scoundrel; I think I shall be able to put matters right. But we must proceed cautiously. The governor is one of those men who do not like to be found out doing the

the wrong thing. He may take it into his head to stand by this Osric Grame."

"We have settled a plan, Jack," said Dave. "I think it will about please you. Have a glass of wine, and take a cigar. We will talk it over, and see what you think of it."

CHAPTER XXVI.

A GAMBLING ROW—THE DUEL—OSRIC GRAME MEETS WITH A KINDRED SPIRIT.

NDER the influence of intoxication men do strange things, and a man can get drunk without strong drink. Osric Grame was intoxicated with the pride of success.

He had triumphed over Daring Dave— he was sure of it— and he went back home resolved upon doing something more. He would get rid of Lina.

A very simple plan came into his head, and he wondered he had not thought of it before.

He would drug her food or wine, and, under the cover of the darkness of night, carry her away to an adjoining cliff and throw her over.

What was more natural than the act of suicide by by one who was mad?

Who could suspect him, or, suspecting him, would

venture to utter their thoughts. With Lina dead and his persistent foe a prisoner he was free.

Ere the morning was past he knew that the Water Sprite was gone, and the Cyclops in pursuit. He was a witness of these things, and joy intoxicated him.

"A fig for the dreams of a woman!" he cried, "and her whispering of Fate. Fate—indeed! A man is the ruler of his own. I have never yet met my match. Bah! I have as yet only encountered children."

There was a small hotel at St. Marie, chiefly used by planters and the military loungers. The law was lax in respect to gambling, and a great deal of it was carried on there.

Osric Grame, having seen the Water Sprite and Cyclops disappear in the distance, went to this hotel, where he found a number of young bloods of the place. The reception he met with did not satisfy him.

They were all a bit offhand, and two or three decidedly cool, notably a young planter named Josef Matadore.

They were playing cards for high stakes, and two or three had been drinking heavily, again notably the young planter named.

"Can I join in?" asked Osric Grame, bringing out a well-filled purse.

"No," replied Josef Matadore, answering for the rest.

"And why not, pray?" asked the pirate, with knitted brow.

"There isn't room for you," was the answer.

"There is room for half a dozen," said Osric Grame, with a tigerish snarl. "I warn you that I shall not stand insult from any of you."

"We want to know more about that sister of yours," said Matadore. "She is no more mad than I am. I met her two hours ago, and she talked sensibly enough. Where do you come from? Who are you?"

"Am I to carry my family history about with me?" demanded Osric Grame.

"You carry your own on your face," said Josef Matadore, coolly; "anyone can read infernal rogue upon it."

Osric Grame drew back a pace, and the attitude was too much like that of a tiger preparing for a spring to be mistaken.

It was an old way of his, practised years before, and from it he had gained the name of the Nevada Tiger.

Two or three of the lookers-on threw themselves between him and the out-spoken Josef; but he tossed them aside as if they had been dolls, and dashed the young fellow to the ground.

There he would have throttled him in his mad fury, for his blood was up, but for the efforts of the whole party.

They tore him away, but not before the table had been overturned, and the things upon it thrown in every direction.

Decanters and glasses were smashed, and the noise brought in the landlord—a mulatto—and a dozen servants of various shades of brown and black.

Quivering with alarm, the landlord begged there would be no more fighting.

"It would be my ruin," he said. "My licence would be taken away by the governor."

"There will be no more fighting HERE," said

Osric Grame. " Is there any man who will stand by me ?"

" I will," replied a middle-aged planter, one of the most dissolute men of the place, named Pradu.

He had a dark record of sin against him, and some terrible stories were told of orgies that had been indulged in by himself and some of his closer friends.

But up to that time he had held on to society by the skin of his teeth.

" Arrange a meeting," said Osric Grame, " in an hour. You will find me at home. My grounds are at the service of Matadore."

" I will meet you anywhere, rogue—thief— PIRATE !" cried the young fellow.

" It isn't fair !" cried another of the guests. " You are no match for him, Matadore."

" It was Matadore who provoked the affair," said Pradu. " If he does not fight I will proclaim him a coward."

" You were always his foe," said the previous speaker, "as well as mine."

It was Matadore's brother—his elder—who spoke thus. His name was Andre.

" Let this be my affair. Josef knows little about fighting. He has only just come back from a college in Europe."

" He should not let his tongue wag so freely," said Pradu ; "and he must meet his man."

" Andre," said Josef, " I beg of you to say no more. The fellow is a scoundrel, and may be more than a match for me ; but I will meet him."

After this no more could be said ; and Andre drew aside with Pradu to make the needed ar-

Osric Grame had already gone, after whispering to his second the word "swords," he, as the insulted party, having the choice.

Ere the hour was up Pradu called upon Osric Grame, whom he found smoking under the verandah with two swords by his side, and told him that the two brothers would speedily follow him.

While he was speaking they appeared, and the whole party adjourned to a quiet, wild part of the grounds.

On their way thither Pradu seized an opportunity to whisper a few words of advice to his principal.

"Prick him only," he said. "It will give him the lesson he wants."

"I mean to KILL him!" was the answer of Osric Grame.

Pradu slightly knitted his brow.

He had not anticipated the affair would end so seriously.

He simply offered his services to curry favour with "The Rajah."

A favourable spot was found; and the swords having been measured and handed to the combatants, the seconds drew aside.

What is murder?

It is for one man to take advantage of the inferior powers of another, and deliberately kill him.

Murder was done by Osric Grame that day.

Josef Matadore was in the pride of early manhood.

He was handsome, honourable, and, a short time before, had a long life ahead of him.

But what cared the Nevada Tiger for all these things?

The moment they crossed swords he knew he had the young fellow at his mercy.

But he did not kill him at once.

That would have been cutting short the joy he felt in his work—eating his pudding at one mouthful.

So he toyed with him—parrying his imperfect thrusts, smiling at his crude handling of the sword, until the desire to kill became irrepressible.

Then, with a movement of his wrist, he turned the other's weapon aside, and drove his own through Matadore's heart.

Not a sound escaped the poor fellow. He fell to the earth with a thud, and lay still.

Andre, with a cry of anguish, rushed up and half-raised his brother's lifeless body.

"Dead!" he wailed. "How shall I bear the tidings to your mother? It will kill her."

"The young dog should have kept his tongue quiet," said Osric Grame.

"Come away!" said Pradu. "Do not insult a a man after you have killed him."

"Dog, did you call him?" cried Andre, shaking his fist at Osric Grame. "He is nobler dead than you are living. He was right. You are all we have suspected. The woman you call your sister has not lied. You are no Rajah—but a pirate, murderer —living on your blood-stained wealth."

"Beware!" cried Osric Grame, threateningly, "or I may lay you out beside him."

"Come away!" said Pradu, impatiently. "Isn't it natural that he should lose his head a little at such a time. Are you mad, too? Does it run through ALL your family?"

The sarcastic tones of the latter remark stung

Osric Grame, but he yielded to his second, and allowed himself to be led away.

"It's a cursed pity you killed him," said Pradu, when they were out of ear-shot. "The Matadores are a popular family. The governor won't like it."

"Hang the governor!" growled Osric Grame.

"That is all very well," said Pradu; "but he is absolute here, and there are laws against duelling which, if winked at occasionally, can be put in force."

"What can they do?"

"Imprison you—try you for murder!"

"Then why, in the fiend's name, didn't you let me kill the other? We could have buried the pair."

"Bah! man. That would have been a wild trick. On my word, I shall soon begin to think you are as mad as your sister. Is it not known all over St. Marie that the duel was to take place?"

Osric Grame did not answer him—nor did he speak again until the house was reached. Then he rang the bell, and, having ordered wine, desired some of the servants to go and help Andre Matadore to carry his brother home.

Two kindred spirits had come together in Pradu and Osric Grame. Ere they had got through the first bottle of wine they were talking confidentially together.

Pradu at last became very candid.

"You are no Rajah," he said; "but I don't think the less of you. I am not at all squeamish. Come, out with it. Why did you come HERE?"

"To enjoy life," replied Osric Grame.

"It is a poor place," said Pradu. "I have been chained to it because I have been a bankrupt for years. I want to get away.   Do you want a good man to help you IN ANY WORK ?"

There was a deep significance in the last three words, and after they had been spoken the precious pair sat for awhile looking steadily at each other.

"Can I get away from here in secret ?" asked Osric Grame at last.

"I might arrange it," replied Pradu ; "but you cannot take this place with you."

"Can I sell it ?"

"Yes ; I will find a customer who will take it—at a price.   It will be better than nothing.   Is it all you have ?"

"No ; I have a big fortune at my back."

"Where is it ?"

"Here.   Come with me.   Drink another glass of wine first."

He uncorked a second bottle, and they each drank a tumblerful.   Then Osric Grame led the way to an upper room in the house, where he slept.

In one corner was a cupboard, locked. He opened the door with a key he carried suspended round his neck, and showed Pradu two chests.

"Open that one," he said, pointing to the nearest.

Pradu raised the lid, and saw that it was almost full of jewels—all loose stones.

"The other chest is like this one," he said. "What is the value of both ?"

"I can only guess at it," said Pradu. "A vast fortune, anyway."

"Well, these are mine ; and if I can only get away —to Europe, say—I could live a glorious life. Pradu, there is enough for two. Will you go with me?"

"I will help you to get away, and share your lot," replied Pradu, drawing a deep breath.

"When ?"

"Between now and to-morrow."

"Meanwhile," said Osric Grame, laying a hand upon his arm, "there is something to be done."

"Yes ; to secure a boat to go on board ship."

"I am not thinking of that. There is the woman I call my sister. She cannot go with us, and I must not leave her behind."

"I hate shedding women's blood," said Pradu.

"You need not do it," answered Osric Grame. "Come here to-night—at twelve, let us say—and you will find a sack under the verandah awaiting you."

"What am I to do with it ?" asked Pradu, white to the lips.

"Carry it to the nearest cliff, and empty the CONTENTS down upon the rocks below."

"Where it will be found ?"

"Let it be found, Pradu. There will be no wounds —nothing to point to murder. Mad people commit suicide. Do you understand ?"

"I do," said Pradu, slowly. "Of a truth, you are a veritable fiend ; but I like you none the less. At twelve I will be here."

Osric Grame closed and locked the door. After that they went back to the room, and finished the second bottle of wine in silence.

Both were thinking, and in brief we give the substance of their thoughts.

Osric Grame thought thus : "He shall serve my turn, and help me to get from here, until an opportunity occurs to cast aside a tool I no longer need."

And this was in Pradu's mind—

"I will help him from here, with all he can take with him, as far from the shore as will give me enough water in which to drown him. Pradu, my boy, you will be rich—rich beyond your wildest dreams."

Surely two spirits more akin never before in this world came together !

CHAPTER XXVII.

THE APPOINTED HOUR—A HEAVY BURDEN— OVER THE PRECIPICE—FACE TO FACE.

MIDNIGHT is the assassin's hour—he likes not the light of day—by instinct he selects it for his darkest work.

Therefore had Osric Grame chosen that hour in which to dispose of the woman whom he once professed to love.

Lina had rooms of her own in the mansion, and there she usually ate and drank, and slept alone.

That night Osric Grame sent her a kindly message, strangely at variance with his late bearing towards her.

" I am weary of my loneliness to-night. May I come to you, if only for a little while ?"

The answer she sent was " Yes."

So he went ; but there was no greeting between them. The room was luxuriously furnished, and, as he sat down upon a velvet-covered couch, he said—

" Lina, I wish there to be an end of the war between us. Let us part. You shall go where you will, taking half my possessions. Will that content you ?"

And again she answered "Yes," and nothing more.

She sat very quiet, with dull eyes, as if her thoughts were far away.

He took out his cigar case, selected a small one, and before lighting it said—

" I assume you do not object.   There was a time when you used to say you liked it."

She raised her eyes, looked at him in a dull way, but said nothing. Osric Grame lit his cigar, and smoked on until a servant appeared to announce that dinner was served in an adjoining chamber.

The pirate arose, tossed his cigar out of the open window, and held out his hand to Lina.

Apparently she did not see it, but walked out ahead of him to the adjoining room, a small apartment in which a table was laid for two.

Everything was of the best—the food, the wine, the dinner service, and the plate.

They sat down facing each other, and the dinner was served.

Not a word was said by either. They ate in silence, Oscar Grame scarce daring to look at the woman he intended to kill ; she, with her eyes upon him, dreamy, and dull as heretofore.

It was a strange feast—if such it can be called.

Osric Grame ate little, and Lina only now and then put a morsel into her mouth in a weird mechanical way. Two servants were in attendance, and they shivered as they passed round the table— not knowing why.

No wine was drank at first ; but, by-and-bye, the pirate took up a bottle, already uncorked, and filled a glass.

from the palm of his hand into it—only a few grains of a colourless powder.

He reached across the table and placed the glass by Lina's plate, and then began to drink himself—steadily.

Glass after glass he poured down his throat ; but Lina left her's untasted. Thus the dinner passed, and dessert was put upon the table.

The servants left the room, glad to get away from the wretched scene.

Osric Grame filled his glass again.

" Lina," he said, " let us drink to each other once. It may be the last time."

" Osric Grame," Lina said—" or shall I call you by your right name ?"

" Osric Grame will serve," he said.

" Yes ; Osric Grame I will drink with you once, and for the last time. You wish to get rid of me ; but I feel THAT WE SHALL SEE THE END OF LIFE TOGETHER. I may go, or be taken away from you, but the mysterious faces that surround us will bring us together again."

" Better friends, I hope," he cried, with an attempt at gaiety.

" Hold out your glass," she said. " Touch ! Why do you hesitate ? It is the sign of goodwill and love."

How strange she looked, with a growing light in her eyes. Hard as he was he shrank from her gaze.

" Touch !" she said, again.

His hand shook as he held out his glass. They clinked with a slight rattling sound, and Lina drew her's back.

she tossed off the wine, and dashed the glass upon the table.

It was shivered into a hundred pieces.

"You may go now," she said, slowly.

He rose up, with great beads of perspiration on his brow. Success had so far attended him ; but would he ever forget her face as he saw it at that moment.

No ! He felt that it would haunt him.

He would fain have recalled the deed ; not because he repented.

He rather feared what would follow.

It is better to be haunted by the living than the dead.

.   .   .   .

Midnight, and with it comes Pradu, to perform his share of the work.

As he comes up under the verandah he looks in and sees nothing waiting for him there, so he passes through the open window and into the room.

Osric Grame is sitting there drinking. He looks up with heavy eyes.

"Who are you? What do you want ?"

"Have you forgotten ?" asks Pradu.

Osric Grame remembers then, and points towards the garden.

"You will find IT there—by the fountain. IT was too near. IT spoke to me."

"Why, man, you have not half a heart in you, after all. Don't take any more wine to-night."

"Go and do your work," mutters Osric Grame. "Then come back to me."

Pradu helps himself to wine, and swaggers out.

Osric Grame creeps to the window, and, looking

forth, sees his new found accomplice lift up a sack with something heavy in it, and throw it across his shoulder.

He settles his burden, and with a strong step walks away.

" The last of her," the pirate mutters—" the last of her !"

" Perhaps !"

He starts violently and looks around him. Was it fancy or a vision ?   If the latter, whose voice ?

Still he stands listening for awhile, and hears nothing.

The footsteps of his accomplice have died away. He is out of sight.   There is a dreadful stillness in the air.   Hark ! Footsteps again coming up the garden.   It must be Pradu returning.

He will be welcome, for Osric Grame feels that if he was to be alone throughout the night that he will go mad.

Nearer come the footsteps, up to the house now. Light, elastic footsteps, such as are heard when eager, hurrying men are abroad.

" It does not sound like Pradu," says the pirate, as he draws back slowly.

What new fear is in his heart ? Why should he now dread the coming of any man ?

All has gone well, surely ?

By this time Lina must be lying dead upon the rocks beneath the cliff.

The tide is out, and the fall must kill her.

Nearer come the footsteps, they are up to the window, and the form of a man stands boldly limned against the darkness.

A fierce cry bursts from the lips of Osric Grame.

It is Daring Dave !

CHAPTER XXVIII.
OSRIC GRAME AND DAVE—A QUICK FLIGHT—THE
FIRE AND THE STORM.

FOR a brief spell of time Osric Grame stood like a statue staring at Daring Dave, who surveyed him with the calm intensity of a foe aware of his ability to overcome him in a struggle.

The latter was the first to break the silence.

"Osric Grame," he said, " AS YOU CALL YOUR-SELF, we meet face to face at last, AND NOT FOR THE FIRST TIME. Vile hound and murderer ! I know you."

"Who are you ?" hoarsely demanded the pirate, "and why do you haunt me ?"

"I haunt you," said Dave, "even as the dead must have done these many years. Yield up yourself to me."

"Never with life," answered the pirate, springing back into the room.

He thrust a hand into his pocket and drew out a revolver. Dave whipped out his sword and dashed at him.

Two shots were fired by Osric Grame, but in his haste his aim was wild. Then, with a roar like that which escapes a furious wild beast at the sight of a hunter, he seized a chair, and, whirling it over his head, aimed a blow at Dave's head.

Again were his destructive efforts futile.

One step back did Dave take, and that slight movement gave the pirate the opportunity he wanted.

A second blow from his strong arm brought down the chandelier filled with wax candles in the middle of the room, and with another vengeful howl he made for the door.

A quick turn of the handle and he was outside, and the door closed again. As Dave threw himself against it he heard the click of the lock, and knew that he was for the moment foiled.

But he was not beaten.

Turning back, he leaped over the ruins of the chandelier, in the midst of which some of the fallen candles were burning, and rushed outside.

There he came suddenly against half-a-dozen men, Captain Fairfield foremost.

They were all panting like men who had been running, and the commander of the lost Cyclops uttered a cry of joy.

"Why did you rush on ahead of us? It was a dangerous thing to do."

"I was burning with haste," replied Dave, "and felt that I must go on. I have seen him, but he has for the moment evaded me. Surround the house, or he may escape."

The men waited for no further command, but broke away in two parties in opposite directions, to carry out his desire.

A moment later a volume of smoke came rolling through the open window.

"See there!" cried Captain Fairfield; "the place is on fire."

The pine-wood floor, dry as tinder, had caught fire as soon as the candles had burned through the thick carpet, and the flames were already spreading with incredible rapidity.

The two men rushed in and tried to stamp out the conflagration, but were soon compelled to retreat before the pungent smoke

As they dashed out again a number of dark servants were seen to run across the lawn shrieking for help.

Alarmed by the arrival of the seamen, their already strained nerves had given way, and without sense or reason, they were fleeing for their lives.

"Come back," cried Jack, "and help to put out the fire."

But they heard him not, or, if hearing, would not heed his command. Like a pack of frightened swine they plunged through the shrubberies and disappeared.

The flames had now spread all over the room. Everything was so dry, and, for the most part, of such inflammable material, that the fire ran around as it would have done in a place soaked in turpentine.

The heavy wood furniture, the numerous hangings, the wooden floor, and light panel walls were all excellent material for rapid burning.

Nobody could save the room, and only the most strenuous exertions with proper appliances could save any portion of the doomed house.

Appliances there were none, and such help as Dave had at his command could be of little service.

All thoughts of immediately capturing Osric Grame must be abandoned.

"Fall back here!" cried Dave to the nearest man.

The word was passed on and the men came running in.

As soon as they had collected around him, Dave bade them seek out the servants' part of the house, and bring all the buckets they could find.

There was water in a fountain close by, which could be utilised to cast upon the fire.

"You can do nothing," said Captain Fairfield.

"I fear not," replied Dave, "but the men can try. It is my business to seek out Osric Grame. He must be in the house still."

There were at least half a score exits from the place, and Dave, sword in hand, moved round from one to the other two or three times, but saw nothing of his foe. By that time he must have escaped or, if hiding in the house, his doom was sealed.

The fire had leaped from room to room, caught the verandah, and ran up to the wooden roof, over which it spread like an ignited powder-train.

Dave's followers had found a few buckets, but they were useless. No exertions on the part of the little band with such miserable appliances could be of any avail.

The place burnt like a badly-built theatre. There was fire from one end to the other in less than a quarter of an hour.

And now a roar of voices was heard in the direction of the town, and the significance of it was readily grasped by the small party.

The populace had caught sight of the fire, and a general alarm was being raised.

In a few minutes the gardens would be swarming with the mixed population of St. Marie.

"My friend," said Captain Fairfield, "we can do no good here, and to be discovered in the place might lead to complications."

"I understand you," replied Dave. "Against my will we must retreat. But that villain has escaped me!"

"Probably to perish—awfully—there!" said Captain Fairfield, solemnly, pointing towards the burning house.

"I hope not," answered Dave. "The account I have against him would be imperfectly settled that way!"

With a keen sense of disappointment in his heart he turned aside, and walked moodily in the direction by which he had come.

The others followed him, and the burning house was speedily left to itself.

But not for long.

Half a minute later Pradu came tearing into the garden, staring wildly at the glowing furnace before him, unable to grasp the portent of the wild scene.

"What does it mean?" he cried. "What devil's work has the Rajah been guilty of?"

But he could not stay there to investigate the matter, for the roar of an advancing crowd fell upon his ears, and he knew that to be discovered there alone might lead to his being questioned in an inconvenient manner.

So he departed also with such haste as the occasion demanded, and once more the fire was left to itself.

But again not for long.

Up from the town poured a motley crowd of rich, and poor, white, black, and brown, well clothed and ragged—a veritable whirlwind of mixed humanity.

The yells of "Fire—Fire!" were deafening, but there was no one to take the lead and attempt to save any portion of the mansion from ruin.

The terrible all-devouring element had obtained complete mastery, and the richly-carved woodwork, of which the house was principally built, and the upholstery were speedily consumed.

No human aid could save it now.

So the spectators made the next best use of their energies and ran round the house, watching the flames, calling out to each other, dancing, leaping, and in a frenzied way enjoying themselves.

The black men and half-castes acted like men possessed.

Not satisfied with the splendour of the spectacle, or subdued in any way by fatigue arising from their wild antics, they ran about the grounds seeking material to add to the fire.

Garden-seats, arches of wood, several small summer-houses were each in turn torn from their moorings, carried up, and with accompanying yells cast into the flames.

Rare plants, and splendid natural exotics, blooming with magnificent flowers, shared the same fate.

It was a revelry of destruction, and for a time no man sought to stay their hands.

But at last the steady tramp, tramp of soldiers was heard, and a company of men with their officers appeared upon the scene.

As cool and collected as on parade, they formed into line, and, spreading out in front of the house, drove back the yelling crowd.

Disorder yielded to discipline and a few necessary hard knocks.

When about a score of the most refractory had been unceremoniously bowled over with the butt-ends of the soldiers' rifles, the rest retreated to a safe distance, and contented themselves with dancing and yelling.

Two more companies of infantry appeared on the scene, but they could do nothing beyond assisting to keep back the crowd.

This they did, and the fire raged on—until the roof, first, and then the walls collapsing, the work of destruction was completed.

A few minutes afterwards it was observed that the sky was black, and the crowd, knowing what was pending, cleared out in double quick time.

Five minutes later a tropical shower began to fall heavily, mercilessly beating out the smouldering remnants of the fire.

In the midst of the storm the soldiers went back to their barracks at the double, drenched to the skin.

Swiftly flared up the fire, and swiftly it was extinguished, so that when, half an hour later, the stars peeped out again, the mansion of Osric Grame was only a mass of black, rain-sodden ruins.

CHAPTER XXIX.

SMOOTHING THE WAY FOR DAVE—OSRIC GRAME AND PRADU—HAUNTED.

NCE more we find Sir Hercules Cherryton at breakfast, but this time alone.

The alarm of the fire had upset the nerves of his lady, and she was having some toast and eggs and a cup of strong tea in bed.

Sir Hercules was himself upset a bit, for in the first place his wife had been very severe upon him for not having had the fire stopped or extinguished or done something with, and in the second place, he had been kept awake half the night by the noises made by the wakeful population.

He was, in short, in a very "crabby" frame of mind.

So when a nigger servant came into the room to say something, he did not give him time to get out his message, but, roaring like a bull, asked—

"What the deuce do you want?"

"Genelman to see you, sar," replied the scared nigger.

"To the deuce with all gentlemen!" bellowed Sir Hercules.

"Naval officer, sar," pleaded the nigger; "cap'en ob de Cyclops."

"Oh! Captain Fairfield," said Sir Hercules. "Perhaps he has captured that notorious pirate fellow. Show him in."

"Yes, Sir Hercules."

The nigger whisked out, glad to get away, and in a minute or so Captain Fairfield appeared.

"Ah! Fairfield, how de do?" said Sir Hercules. "Have you breakfasted?"

"No, sir, thanks; but—"

"Sit down and have some. You can talk as well as eat."

Captain Fairfield was not averse to good fare, so he sat down, and at the bidding of his host helped himself to some game pie.

"Now, Fairfield," said Sir Hercules, "your news. You've got the fellow, of course?'

"What fellow, Sir Hercules?"

"The pirate."

"There has been no pirate."

"What! did you miss him?"

"I pursued the craft as desired, and found it was

an English gentleman's yacht, armed to protect itself, as its owner has been sailing in unknown seas."

"Hum! that's all right in a way. You found his papers all square?"

"I know his family and can vouch for him. For the present he is sailing *incognito*."

"What!" exclaimed Sir Hercules, "is it one of the princes?"

"Not exactly," replied Captain Fairfield, smiling, "but I will ask you to take my guarantee that he is all right."

"Fairfield, I will do it with pleasure."

"Thank you, Sir Hercules."

There was a short silence, Captain Fairfield making the best of his time in getting outside a good breakfast before he went into more serious matters.

"Sir Hercules," he said, at length, "I am sorry to say I bring bad news."

"Eh! what?" exclaimed the governor, alarmed. "You don't mean to say I am to be recalled, or—"

"No, Sir Hercules; it will not affect your personal interests, but it is a serious matter. The Cyclops is lost."

The governor laid down his knife and fork, and for a moment it seemed as if his eyes would come right out of his head.

"Lost—the Cyclops!" was all he could say.

"Yes," said Captain Fairfield, solemnly, "she struck upon a reef not marked in the chart, formed, I should say, since the chart was made. Worse than all, nearly every hand was lost. The few that were saved, including myself, owe our lives to the gallant people of the Water Sprite."

"The supposed pirate?"

" Yes, Sir Hercules."

" Fairfield," said the governor, after a silence, "this is indeed a bad business, and you will have to stand a court-martial. You ought to have known where you were going."

" I was commanded to follow a certain craft—and I did so."

Sir Hercules made no further comment, but listened patiently, though not without emotion, to the captain's account of the disaster and his report concerning the Water Sprite.

About six o'clock in the evening that vessel, having been skilfully extricated from her dangerous position, arrived off St. Marie.

Captain Fairfield went out in a boat to meet her, and on his informing Daring Dave that he had satisfactorily explained matters to the authorities, the pair came ashore.

Jack remained on board in command, but some of the men obtained a few hours' leave, among them Crupper and Vunder Fuie, the former insisting upon taking the " whale-and-winkle-phone," in order to " make the natives sit up with good music," as he expressed it.

·   ·   ·   ·   ·   ·

While the excitement of the arrival of the Water Sprite had drawn nearly all the population to the beach, Osric Grame and Pradu were hard at work on the south side of the ruins of the pirate's mansion, endeavouring to recover the treasure from the débris.

They toiled on without speaking for a time, only pausing now and then to listen if any one were approaching.

Presently the spade struck against some hard substance, and Pradu uttered a cry of exultation.

Together they worked awhile with the strength of burning excitement, and a portion of a strong iron-bound chest, a little singed, but otherwise unharmed, was laid bare.

At the moment this was done, the face of Lina, horribly white and weird-looking, appeared at an opening in the ruins.

Osric Grame at the same instant happened to look around and it instantly disappeared.

The pirate staggered against his companion and grasped him by the shoulder.

" What ails you ?" demanded Pradu.

"There—there— HER face !" gasped Osric Grame.

"Oh! that's all foolery," cried Pradu, losing colour himself ; "it CAN'T be."

He cast down the spade, and, rushing to the opening, looked around.

" There is nobody here," he said ; "you must have fancied it."

"I did not," replied the pirate. "Pradu, tell me the truth. It doesn't matter if you deceived me before. Did you throw her over the cliff ?"

"I dropped her down," Pradu answered, "and heard the heavy fall of the body on the rocks below. I swear it."

"Haunted—haunted !" muttered Osric Grame, with a fearful look around him.

"Pooh—rubbish !" said Pradu ; "there are no such things as ghosts. It's fancy. All goes well with us. We'll cover up this chest and come for it after dark, and then away, over the sea, to another land, where we'll make amends for all we've gone through here."

Osric Grame did not answer him.

He only stared ahead, and continued to mutter to himself—

"Haunted—haunted!"

CHAPTER XXX.

AMONG FRIENDS—AN HOUR'S GAMBLING—A MAN OF LUCK—THE IMPENDING DUEL.

WHEN people go to Rome they are supposed to do as Rome does In other words, the traveller has, more or less, to fall into the habits of the peoples with whom he comes in contact.

Thus, when Dave got ashore, and found himself in the company of English officers and leading planters, he naturally joined in their amusements.

"To-night," said Captain Fairfield, "you are at liberty to do as you please. But to-morrow I must introduce you to the governor, and then you must put up with a few hours' formality."

Dave found himself in very amiable society. His youth, good looks, and dashing bearing instantly won him many friends.

All looked on him with favour, and his being *incog.* put a spice of romance on him in the eyes of men who had had no knowledge of his really romantic history.

No impertinent questions were asked him as a

matter of course. The system of vulgar prying, such as Americans freely indulge in, is not adopted by Englishmen.

He was introduced as Captain Dave, and by that name he was addressed.

A number of the men to whom he was introduced hospitably formed themselves into a committee of reception, and invited him to the chief hotel to dinner.

He accepted the invitation, and the dinner was ordered. While it was being prepared they adjourned to the billiard-room, which speedily filled with the notabilities of the place.

Gambling is a great evil without a doubt, but it seems to be in the very heart of men, and especially so in such places as the Island of St. Marie.

The planters and officers at once plunged into their favourite pursuit.

"You don't play?" said one of the young planters, in whom Dave had shown a little interest.

It was Andre Matadore, the brother of the murdered Josef—for murdered he was, under the guise of a duel.

Andre was a handsome fellow, only a few days before the life and spirit of the place, but now wearing a quietly-sad expression on his face.

He did not talk about his dead brother—a sure sign of his feeling his loss with terrible keenness—but went about his affairs as usual; not with the spirit of old, but in a listless, mechanical way.

Nobody ventured to speak to him of his sorrow, for they knew it would be distasteful; nor did they name "the Rajah," who was supposed to have perished in the burning house, in his presence.

Andre did not believe he was dead, and in his

heart looked for the time when they would meet again.

It is true he did not know why the "Rajah" should be in hiding ; but he was certain that for some reason he was skulking about the island.

All discussion about Osric Grame and his sister, both missing, was discontinued when he appeared.

"You do not play ?" he said to Dave.

"No," was the reply ; "why should I ?"

"Well, to win," said Andre.

"What pleasure would that give me ?" asked Dave ; "I have already a great deal more money than I want. I do not think I can ever spend it."

Andre looked at him with curiosity and just a wee bit of envy.

"Is it so ?" he said.

Dave smiled, and hesitated a moment before replying.

"It's rather caddish to talk about one's money," he said, "but I am very rich ; I don't know what I am worth."

"Then why not go in for the pleasure of LOSING ?" suggested Andre ; "one must do something with money."

"To whom shall I lose it ?"

"Not to me. But here comes a man who would not mind getting hold of some of it ; and he wants it, too."

It was Pradu to whom he referred, who at that moment sauntered into the room with a defiant air.

He knew how little he would be welcome among these men, but as yet he was OF them, and except at the risk of a quarrel and a duel, they could not cut him dead.

He stood for a moment in the doorway, glancing

round the room. Then his face brightened as his eyes fell upon Dave.

Although they had never met before, there was a conscious look of RECOGNITION to be observed in both.

Pradu, a few minutes later, sauntered up to Dave and raised his hat.

"I believe I have the honour of addressing the captain of the Water Sprite?" he said.

Dave bowed.

"May I be so bold as to give you a welcome to St. Marie?" continued Pradu.

What could Dave say, but express in as few words as possible his sense of the man's courtesy, all the while feeling a deep repugnance towards him?

The feeling would have been intensified if he had known that the man had come there with the deliberate intention of taking advantage of a favourable opportunity, if it offered, to assassinate him.

He had promised Osric Grame that it should be done. He offered himself as a friendly agent for the deed to blind the "Rajah," at the same time not knowing why he should desire the assassination of the young Englishman.

"It is simply because I hate ALL Englishmen," said Osric Grame, "and this one made himself offensive to me in India."

Pradu took a seat beside Dave, and entered into conversation with him. Andre, with a dry smile on his lips, sat on the other side of our hero, silent and watchful.

Ere long Pradu's ruling passion prompted him to suggest play.

"Just a game of ecarté to while away the time."

Tables for play were ranged all round the room, and as Dave indifferently assented, Pradu placed one between them, and produced a pack of cards.

"Are there none to be had in the establishment?" quietly asked Dave.

"Oh ! yes, if you wish it," replied Pradu, with a flushed face.

"It is not the usual thing—at home—for players to provide their own cards," said Dave.

A delighted look sprang into Andre's eyes. He saw that Pradu had no raw novice to deal with, but one who would probably hold his own against the professional gambler.

An attendant was summoned and cards brought, a new pack, with the wrapper unbroken.

Dave opened the neat little parcel, and finding that the cards were plain, shuffled and passed them to Pradu.

"What shall we play for?" he asked.

"What you like," answered Pradu.

"It is a matter of indifference to me."

"I would rather leave it to you."

"Well, suppose we say five hundred pounds a game?" said Dave, coolly.

Pradu started, and some of the colour fled from his cheeks. It was higher than he had ever played in his life, and if he lost more than he possessed— Bah ! how could he lose with such a fledgeling ?

"It is rather high," he said ; "but to please you, yes."

In less than a minute a whisper of the heavy gambling about to be indulged in passed round the room, and more than half the company abandoned their own game to gather round Dave's table to watch the play.

It seemed a pity that one so young and inexperienced as Dave should fall into the hands of an old hawk like Pradu.

So the watchers whispered among themselves, but no man dared to interfere. It would be entirely at variance with the gambler's code of honour.

Dave was no gambler, or ever had been, but he had many a time played a friendly game of ecarté at home, and if not an adept at it, had at least a shrewd idea of the way to play.

He had one great advantage over Pradu, and that was, if he lost he could pay.

Pradu could not, and he knew that if he lost and did not pay at once an unpleasant scene might occur.

He was already on the list of doubtfuls, and any attempt to evade his liabilities would lead to his violent expulsion from the room.

Old gamester as he was, his lips quivered and his hand shook as he dealt the cards.

Dave looked at his hand.

"Do you beg?" asked Pradu.

"No, and I mark the king," answered Dave.

Well, we need not dwell upon the scene. Luck, assisted by coolness and fair play, contrived to win for Dave five games right off the reel.

No money passed as the stakes were so large, but at the end of each game Pradu gave an I. O. U. for five hundred pounds.

"Everything goes in my favour," said Dave ; "I think we had better play no more to-night. To-morrow you can have your revenge."

"I want to go on," said Pradu, hoarsely.

"You cannot," interposed Andre, "there goes the dinner gong."

Dave rose, and, laying a hand upon the I. O. U.'s, pushed them over to Pradu.

"Give me a cheque for the whole," he said.

"Let it be till to-morrow," said Pradu, with pallid cheeks and a quaver in his voice.

"As you will," calmly answered Dave.

"Pardon me," said Andre, "but that won't do. This man has no means of paying such a sum, and to-morrow never comes."

"That is so—that is so," cried a score voices.

The opportunity so long sought had come at last. Pradu, the gambler, was at the mercy of those around him.

"Gentlemen," he said, "I swear I will be here with the money to-morrow, and stake more to gain my revenge."

But they only laughed,

"Where are you to get the money from?" asked half-a-dozen voices.

"It has been a case of heads he wins and tails Captain Dave loses," said one of the officers.

Pradu turned in the direction of the speaker with a ferocious air.

"You lie!" he said.

The officer stepped out from the crowd and gave Pradu a back-handed blow on the chest.

"That is my answer," he said.

Pradu put his hand into his pocket, but drew it out again—empty. It was not the place to attempt assassination; but he would kill the officer fairly.

"Is there anybody here who will stand by me?" he asked. "It won't be a long affair; we can settle it in ten minutes."

"Where?" asked Dave.

"Here," answered Pradu.

"Pooh ! monsieur," said Andre ; " you know better than that.   Send your man here to-morrow. But, meanwhile, what of your debt to Captain Dave ?"

" It is of no consequence—let him go," said Dave.

" He will never pay !" cried a score voices.

" If he is a blackleg," said Dave, " he should be kicked from the room."

" Who will do it ?" asked Pradu, fiercely.

" *I* will," said Dave, moving towards him. " You came here in search of me.   WHO SENT YOU ?   I have heard to-day of a duel in which you played the part of a second.   Are you the tool of the RAJAH, as you were in the other affair ?"

Dave had lowered his voice, so that Pradu alone caught the full sense of the words.   The dismayed gambler began to back slowly.

" I know nothing of this *Rajah*," he said, " more than anyone here.   I came here to have half an hour's amusement.   I have lost—strangely ; I do not understand.   It was luck beyond fair play, and—"

Dave sprang upon him and struck him between the eyes, knocking him down as if he had been shot.

" You dare to impute unfair play to me ?" he cried.

" I do," cried Pradu ; " I saw you sleeve the king once—"

He was interrupted by a chorus of dissentient voices, in the midst of which he got upon his feet.

" I am one against many," he said, " and I must put up with anything."

" Gentlemen," said Dave, " I ask of you as a favour to let this man go."

" I want satisfaction for the blow you have dealt me," cried Pradu.

"You shall have it," replied Dave.

"Where and when?"

"Choose yourself."

"Here and now," said Pradu.

"Pardon me," interposed Andre, "there is the second gong for dinner; we cannot let it spoil. Pradu, get a second from somewhere; no doubt you will be able to secure a man from the riff-raff of the town. Captain Dave shall be at your service at eight o'clock."

"Where?" hissed Pradu.

"Here; and the weapons—Captain Dave, it is your choice," said Andre.

"Swords," replied Dave, briefly.

And then, the third rumbling of the gong falling on their ears, there was a general move in the direction of the dining saloon.

Pradu remained behind, and as soon as he was alone he touched a bell and ordered a bottle of wine of a responding negro attendant.

Then he sat down and lighted a cigar.

"Was ever so scurvy a trick played by Fate?" he muttered. "At eight I had appointed to meet the Rajah—at eight I must be here to kill this unfledged cub, who has the luck of the fiend on his side. I cannot shirk the meeting, for I intend to return here rich, and put these arrogant curs to shame. I think I may keep the Rajah waiting half an hour. Yes, I will do so."

At this moment a burst of laughter was heard in the direction of the dining-room.

"Ah! laugh now," he hissed, with a shake of his clenched hand; "there will be mourning before midnight among you—for I'll kill him, or may a curse rest on the name of Pradu!"

CHAPTER XXXI.

VUNDER FULE AND CRUPPER DINE ASHORE—
THEY HEAR OF SOMETHING INTERESTING AND
RATHER TROUBLING.

EXT to the delights of a fight at sea nothing pleases a Jack Tar so much as a bit of a fling ashore, and Daring Dave's men were no exception to the general body of sea-faring men.

They were very liberally supplied with pocket-money, and, with the exception of an adjuration from Mr. Pegs "not to make bigger fools of themselves than they could help," they were practically free to do as they pleased.

The seamen kept together, but Crupper and Vunder Fule, with that precious musical instrument, went off by themselves.

"We'll have a good dinner somewheres," said Crupper, "and as soon as it is dark we will liven up the place with some dulcimore music."

"You better play him," said Vunder Fule, rather sadly ; "it is all gone from my heart."

"Oh ! nonsense," said Crupper ; "as soon as you hear the sweet voice again you'll go back to your old love."

Dining-places were rather scarce at St. Marie—indeed, the only place where a decent dinner could be got was at the hotel, and thither they, after some dubious discussion, wended their way.

They arrived there shortly before Daring Dave and his new friends put in an appearance.

To Crupper's astonishment they were received as honoured guests, and the enormous brass musical terest to the half-dozen nigger attendants in the dining-room.

Vunder Fule placed it on a chair, and the sable waiters seized every opportunity to stoop down and peer into its enormous bell-shaped bottom.

Vunder Fule rather resented this, and while something to eat was being prepared he showed a growing uneasiness, which Crupper observed, and at last undertook to dispel.

"I'll stop their dern curiosity," he said; "it's nuthin to them what is inside it."

An opportunity for checking the unseemly prying soon offered itself.

The most persistent nigger of all, a wiry white-wooled old man, came up for about the seventh time, and stooping down with his hands upon his knees, peered into the brass tunnel of the trombone.

At first he stood about a foot away. Then with a jerk he put his head a little closer. Finally he worked his way up until his face was fairly inside it.

This was just the position for Crupper's purpose.

Rising quietly from his chair, he softly crept up behind the nigger and gave him a kick that shot him forward like an arrow from a bow.

His head was fairly driven into the instrument to the shoulders, wedging it upon him as tight as the celebrated fixture worn by the "man with the iron mask."

The startled nigger fell over the chair, and after a brief but wild struggle got upon his feet with the trombone sticking up like a chimney-pot upon his head.

In blind terror he began to run about the room, upsetting several chairs and a table, his terrified fellow-servitors fleeing in all directions.

Crupper, with his characteristic coolness, speedily put an end to the scene.

First he put out his foot, and tripped up the aged nigger, catching hold of the instrument as he fell.

Then he called on Vunder Fule to assist him to extricate the unfortunate man.

"Ketch hold of his feet!" he cried, "by the heels and hold on. I'll do the jerking out."

Two or three short, sharp movements released the nigger, who came out of his temporary imprisonment with bulging eyes and his wool straight with terror.

"What yer mean by intruding yourself in there?" sternly demanded Crupper.

"Someborry shove or kick me dar," replied the nigger, "and dat a ting not to be done to Claudius Buckleberry Crank for nuffin. Who do dat, I ask?"

"If I was you," said Crupper, "I shouldn't stand no nonsense from them other niggers."

It was certainly evading a direct reply, but it was not untruthful, although it inferred that the "other niggers" were the culprits.

Claudius Buckleberry Crank was head waiter there and usually kept his dignity. For a junior waiter to play a trick upon him was the most daring piece of insolence ever perpetrated in this world.

So Claudius Buckleberry Crank laid himself out to stop that sort of thing for good and all, and when they came back one by one he, to Crupper's great amusement, gave each a kick ON THE SHINS.

"You do dat again!" he cried. "What you mean by projecterating a genelman nigger into dat brass ting, eh?"

"We not do it, sah!" roared one of the niggers.

"Don't you wase no lyin' words on me, Poulson

Crucible Dabs," cried Claudius Buckleberry Crank. "Dat worse dan de riginal outburse ob crime. Dat'll do now. Get de dinner for dese genelmen— smart! You hear, or I boun' to get again in de nebbyhood ob your shins. D'ye mark, you scropions?"

The "scropions" knew the old man too well to argue with him, but hastened to get in the dinner, which Crupper and Vunder Fule were really in need of.

While one waited on the guests the rest were occupied in preparing two long tables close by, and from their chatter Crupper gathered that they were intended for Daring Dave and his friends.

So he hurried up with his own meal and bade Vunder Fule do the same.

By-and-bye other niggers came in, bringing with them little bits of gossip from the billiard-room.

Crupper listened to it, and by degrees got possession of a very good outline of what had transpired there.

The finishing part of it he heard as he was settling with Claudius Buckleberry Crank, and it rather discomposed him.

"Come out, Vunder Fule," he said. "I don't want the cap'en to see us here."

Outside of the hotel there were a number of seats, the climate favouring much sitting out of doors.

Crupper took possession of one as far removed from the entrance to the hotel as possible.

"You heard that, Vunder Fule?" he said. "The cap'en is going to fight a duel?"

"Yes, zat is so," said Vunder Fule, complacently.

"And in that place, too? What a rowdy lot they must be."

"Ah ! yes."

"I say, Vunder Fule, do you think they will give him fair play?" whispered Crupper. "I don't like the lot I see about here. There's a KNIFEY look about them."

"Ze cap'en gif dem all of English BEANS," said Vunder Fule, serenely. "Vat you tink of trouble for?"

"Well, I don't like the look of it," said Crupper ; "but I don't see that I can do anything."

There was one thing he did not know, and that was the hour appointed for the duel.

Anyway, it must be after dinner, so he wandered away with Vunder Fule into the straggling streets of the town.

It was now dark, and there was no gas at St. Marie. What lighting as there was came from the stars and such lamps as the better classes chose to hang outside their doors.

There were, however, many people abroad, principally niggers and half-castes, many of them on courting bent.

Crupper was inclined to be low in spirits, but his mercurial disposition could not remain under such an influence for any length of time.

Turning into a bye-street, he saw ahead of him two niggers, one of either sex. Their close proximity and slow walk revealed the fact that they were in the thick of love's young dream.

The gentleman wore an old soldier's coat, check trousers down to his knees, and a well-worn tall hat, which had once belonged to some Englishman.

His feet were without boots, probably on account of the size, which would have entailed a special make at a considerable outlay.

As for the lady, she was as gorgeous as a short red gown, blue shawl, and old palm hat garnished with real vegetables and flowers could make her.

Neither were conscious of anything in the wide world but themselves.

"Here, Vunder Fule," said Crupper, "I must cheer myself up somehow. Give me that 'ere whale-and-winkle-phone."

Vunder Fule handed him the instrument, and, Crupper, holding it ready for action, crept softly up to the lovers, drawing in a deep breath, so as to have plenty of wind for a grand and glorious outburst.

Holding the instrument so that the wide end was close to one of the gentleman nigger's ears, he poured into it all the breath he had at his command.

The result was one loud, hideous, ear-splitting, overwhelming note.

He expected great results, but nothing like what ensued.

The lover leaped two feet in the air, bore sideways, and falling heavily, rolled upon his back and lay upon the ground bereft for the time of motion

As for the lady, she uttered such a scream as never escaped anything but a negress or a wild cat in a trap, and jerking her head up, tossed off her hat. Then a sudden limpness overcame her, and with a very audible flop she sat down upon her head-gear, dislocating all its outside arrangements and ruining what remained of the hat to spoil.

Crupper was almost as much taken aback as the objects of his musical joke, but he did not quite lose his head.

"Here, Vunder Fule," he said, "ketch hold of this thunder-and-lightning-phone, while I bear a hand to assist these two mortiful beings in distress."

Vunder Fule took charge of the instrument, in no way moved, save that he felt a little glow of satisfaction at finding that it had the power to lay two mortals in the dust, and Crupper, gallantly kneeling over the lady, asked if he could be of any service to her?

By way of answer she gave him a box on the ear with a hand approximating in size to an ordinary frying-pan, and the valiant joker immediately found himself surveying a chaotic mass of fireworks.

Stepping back, he tripped upon the nigger, who, in a mechanical, dreamy way, was making an effort to rise.

Crupper's weight sent him down again, and the gallant seaman's body falling upon the centre of his stomach, acted upon him as it would have done upon an india-rubber toy with a small musical instrument fixed in it.

A most awful squeak, short, sharp, but thrilling, escaped the hapless darkey, and then he was apparently done with for ever.

At that moment half-a-dozen young nigger sparks, on their way to a ball given by one of their friends, came round the corner.

It is needless to describe their attire in detail, on the whole it was brilliant, and, to the ordinary eye, bewildering in its odds-and-ends beauty.

They saw one of their race being set upon by a white man, and a small one, a seaman too, and the fires of wrath, engendered by a sense of being as free as anybody else, and freer, leaped up in their hearts.

"Golly, misters," cried one, "what dis? Lonzo Alexandry Popbottle Jukes bein' murdered! Gib de ugly white man a squashing."

Immediately all lowered their heads, and in orthodox nigger-fighting fashion charged at the daring white man who had ventured to assault one of their noble emancipated race.

———

CHAPTER XXXII.

CRUPPER AND VUNDER FULE STILL ON THE SPREE —THE DUEL AND WHAT FOLLOWED.

RUPPER still had his wits about him, and saw them coming, so scrambled to his feet just in time to escape the half-dozen human battering-rams.

The majority of them fell over their fallen brother, but two went on ahead across the street, until they were brought up short by their heads colliding with the wall of an opposite house.

This had the effect of stimulating their wits, and with wrathful howls, they wheeled around and got ready for a second charge.

More niggers appeared, and three or four half-castes—all, by their dress, evidently on their way to the ball.

"Look out, Vunder Fule!" cried Crupper. "Follow me."

He wasted no time in parleying, but rushed at

the approaching party, thinking it were better to
return by the way he came.

Unluckily they saw him coming, and being strong
in numbers, closed in upon him and Vunder Fule.

"Hit out!" cried Crupper.

Hitting out not being in the line of the niggers,
they jumped upon him and Vunder Fule, tearing
and clawing at them like so many tigers, and the
fight soon assumed a desperate aspect.

Luckily help was at hand in the form of the other
Jack Tars, who, arm-in-arm, passed the end of
the street, roaring out the well-known sea song—
"In the Bay of Biscay, oh!" One of their number
espied Crupper and Vunder Fule in trouble, and with
a loud whoop, came to the rescue.

The others followed, and in half-a-dozen seconds
the niggers were in full flight.

They were allowed to go, and the lover and his
lady being sufficiently recovered to join the retiring
party, the victors soon had the street to themselves.

"I was afraid, Vunder Fule," said Crupper, "that
your larking would get us into trouble. But never
mind; I like a man of spirit, even if now and then he
do go a bit too far."

Vunder Fule, being engaged in restoring his
smoking-cap, which had been knocked off in the
scuffle, to his head, made no reply.

Perhaps experience had taught him that it would
not have helped very much towards clearing matters,
so he complacently followed the Jack Tars, who
resumed their song and journey to the beach, with
the intention of returning to the Water Sprite.

But suddenly Crupper thought of the coming
duel between his captain and another, and he men-
tioned it to the men, at the same time pointing out

that it was the duty of one and all to be somewhere near to see fair play.

Need we say that the men fell in with his views? and together they wended their way back to the hotel.

The windows of the billiard-room were lighted up, and on the sill of one of them was seated a boy-nigger eagerly peering in.

"What's the matter, young un?" asked Crupper.

"Two genelmen going to fight, sar," was the reply.

Crupper nimbly slipped up to his side, and, as there were no blinds drawn, easily saw what was going on.

Ranged round the room, in perfect order, were a number of officers forming a ring.

In the centre stood Daring Dave and Pradu, sword in hand, about to begin the duel, as arranged.

The whole thing was so orderly that Crupper fel he had no call to interfere, but there could be no harm in his waiting to watch the scene.

As there were two other windows there was plenty of room for more spectators, and the seamen got into positions of vantage.

Vunder Fule alone remained in the street, calmly looking about him as if he had no interest in the matter.

"Tell me," he said, "ven ze cap'en kill him, zen I play ze 'Dead March.'"

"All right," said Crupper, "I'll give you the tip. There they go. The cap'en's as cool as a cucumber."

In the room there was complete silence, and the sailors, being quiet, too, the grating of the swords.

as the combatants began their preliminary play,
could be plainly heard.

Crupper was no longer uneasy.

He was a judge of swordsmanship, and he saw
that Daring Dave could hold his own, and more.

"It'll all be over in three minutes," he said to
himself.

And so it might have been but for an act of the
desperate Pradu.

He, like Crupper, soon discovered that he was
fighting with one who was his master, and feeling
himself pressed back, he suddenly drew a revolver
and fired at Dave.

The shot missed its mark, but struck one of the
spectators, a planter, who fell heavily to the floor.

Immediately all was confusion, and Pradu,
revolver in hand, dashed towards the door.

As those near him were not prepared for this
onslaught they yielded for the moment, and the
desperado, reaching the door, dashed out.

"That won't do, my lad!" cried Crupper, leaping
down.

He ran to the front entrance of the hotel, and was
ust in time to meet Pradu as he was rushing out.

The pair collided, and Crupper, who could box
like a champion light-weight, dealt Pradu a stinging
blow on the cheek, following it up with one on the
side of the head, which laid the scoundrel out upon
the ground, bewildered and breathless.

The other sailors were now on the spot, and immediately secured the ruffian, utilising his own
neckerchief to secure his hands.

The next moment a number of the spectators of
the duel came pouncing out in pursuit.

When they saw that Pradu was secured they

uttered exultant shouts, and took possession of him.

"He belongs to us," they said. "Leave us to deal with him."

"It's all right," said Crupper; "I don't want any more of the job. Where's the cap'en?"

Dave was just coming out, and, on seeing Crupper, asked what he was doing there. Having received a brief account of what had been done, he gave Crupper an approving tap upon the shoulder, thanked him, and told him to get on board.

"I shall return in about an hour," he said. "Ask Mr. Pegs to send a boat for me."

Crupper, now thoroughly restored in spirits, bade the men follow him, and walked away with a jaunty step.

"You may play up, Vunder Fule," he said. "Let us have some of the liveliest parts of the 'Winkle and the Whale.'"

Vunder Fule, for the first time for many days, burst out with his favourite melody, filling the air with strains that had rather a trying effect upon the hearers until the sounds died away in the distance.

And now a very serious part of the drama was about to be enacted.

The man shot by Pradu was not dead; but he was very seriously injured, and a fitting punishment must be dealt out to the offender.

It was to take a very peremptory form, which Daring Dave would have no share in—nor the English officers either.

They asked that Pradu might be sent to prison and tried in the ordinary way; but the planters said—"No."

"There are so many ways for him to escape the

punishment he deserves," they argued. " Leave him to us."

So Dave, who really had no voice in the matter, turned away; but ere he had gone far Pradu cried for him to come back.

"I have something to tell you," he said; " it is about the Rajah."

Dave stopped and looked back at him.

"You can tell me what you please," he said; "but I cannot interfere on your behalf."

"Then I will tell you nothing," said Pradu, sullenly.

"He cannot tell me more than I have believed all along," thought Dave. " Osric Grame is alive. It surely will not be a difficult matter to find him."

With his English friends he returned to the hotel, and the planters hurried Pradu away to a spot at the back of the hotel where there was a plot of ground fairly well lighted up by the rays of lamps cast from the windows.

The man who held him tightest was Andre Matadore.

"You played a part in the murder of my brother," he said, "and on you shall fall my first blow of vengeance."

"Your brother fell in fair fight," said Pradu.

"You knew he had no chance with that villain," said Andre, fiercely. "Enough. I will talk to you no more."

The intention of the planters was to lynch the would-be murderer, and they were not prepared for a proposition which Andre made to them.

"Give the brute a chance for his life," he said. " I will fight him."

"Why should you risk your life?" they asked.

"I do not risk it," said Andre, calmly. "I shall kill him as surely as he is a knave and a murderer."

Pradu heard the proposition with a feeling akin to relief, but he was not sure if he overcame Andre that the others would let him go.

"Why should I fight," he said, "if I am to be hanged afterwards?"

"If you prove victor," said Andre, "I trust you will be allowed to go free. I ask you, friends, that it shall be so."

They began to murmur, but he stopped them.

"It is as the request of a man who is dying," he said.

There was a little more expostulating debate, but eventually they yielded. An assent to the proposition was given, and Andre chose the weapons.

"I am like my poor brother was—not skilled in the use of the sword," he said. "I choose pistols."

"Have I no voice in the matter?" asked Pradu.

"None!" was the stern answer.

They loosened his bonds, and men resolved to shoot him down if he attempted to fly were posted around.

"Ten paces" said Andre.

The ground was measured out, and the two men put in their places.

Pradu shook like a leaf.

"He will kill me," he thought, "and away goes all my dreams of wealth. What a fool I was to undertake that affair for the Rajah! May he fall in the hands of his enemies and suffer a thousand deaths!"

They gave him a revolver with one charge only in it. Andre had the same.

" Are you ready ?" asked one of the men.

Andre alone answered " Yes."

Pradu, before the word was given, raised his weapon and fired.

The shot missed, and he cast his weapon to the ground.

It was his intention to run, but his strength failed him.

He could only stand and stare at his opponent, rocking slowly on his feet.

" It is my turn now," said Andre, calmly.

He took his turn, looking steadily for a moment or two at the doomed man.

Then with a quick movement he raised the weapon and fired.

Just for the fraction of a second it seemed as if he had missed, for Pradu still kept his feet.

But the aim had been true—the bullet had gone straight to his heart, taking away his worthless life, and slowly he bent forward, finally falling with a heavy thud upon his face—dead !

CHAPTER XXXIII.

OSRIC GRAME AND HIS TREASURE—FLIGHT—A DISCOVERY AT SEA.

YING close in shore was a fishing-boat, broad in the beam and able to rough a voyage at sea.

It was the property of a half-caste native, who would often go away in it with a crew of three or four men, for weeks at a time, visiting distant islands, fishing and trading. This was the vessel Pradu had finally selected for his flight from St. Marie.

He had a boat of his own, and at first intended to use it, but it was of light build, and would, in all probability, come to grief in a storm.

The skipper of this boat bore the name of Wakeling. He was a fairly honest man, and knew nothing of the plans of Pradu, which were, in brief, to shoot Osric Grame at a fitting moment, and carry off the treasure.

He told Wakeling that he wished to get away from his creditors with some old family plate, all be had left in the world, and promised to pay him well when he landed him at Jamaica or Cuba.

But, as we have seen, Pradu and his plans came to grief, and Osric Grame was in a bit of a fix.

He was at the appointed spot at the hour named

by Pradu, and waited for him in a state of growing impatience until nine o'clock.

Then he began the work of unearthing the chests alone, occasionally pausing to listen for the expected footstep of his associate.

Ten o'clock came, and he, of course, did not arrive. A deadly fear overcame Osric Grame. He felt sure that something had happened to Pradu, or that he had betrayed him to his foes.

At any moment they might come and pounce upon him, and he felt as nervous as a woman.

Recent events had shaken him, and he was no longer the man he had been.

Osric Grame, the bold pirate, had become a coward.

But there was one sustaining power in him, and that was avarice.

He would hold on to his wealth while he had life.

There were three chests, heavy enough ; but not too heavy for a strong man to carry or drag along.

If he could get them down to one of the caves at the bottom of his garden, he could hide them until an opportunity arrived for him to get away.

The one chosen was about a hundred yards from the house, of no great depth, but with several hollows in its walls in which the chests could be put away.

A few stones and some sand would close them in.

He succeeded in getting the boxes thither, and in hiding them from ordinary prying eyes. A further assurance of the safety of his treasure lay in the fact that the cave had an uncanny legend of a ghost attached to it, and none of the lower orders of

Having done his work successfully, he sauntered down towards the town, hoping under the cover of darkness to escape recognition, and, perhaps, he might hear something of Pradu.

Ere he wandered far he came upon Wakeling in eager discussion about the very subject most likely to interest him—the two duels, and the death of Pradu.

"So unlucky for me," said Wakeling, "for I was to have taken him to Jamaica, and been well paid for it."

Shortly after he walked away, and Osric Grame, who had succeeded in escaping recognition, followed him.

It was on the outskirts of the little pier of the harbour that he overtook him.

"One word with you," he said, touching the man upon the shoulder.

Wakeling turned round, and after a hard stare at him, he said—

"It's the Rajah."

"Yes," said Osric Grame; "but you seem more astonished than you need be."

"They have been saying, Rajah, that you were burnt to death."

"I had a narrow escape, and as I am tired of this place, I should be glad to get out without the bother of leave-taking. Instead of Pradu, you may take me to Jamaica."

"But, Rajah—"

"Now, Wakeling, it is only a whim. I will pay you double the sum Pradu promised you. Ask no questions, my man, but make money while you can."

said Wakeling. "There is so little wind that we must wait for the turn of the tide."

"What hour will it serve?"

"Three in the morning, Rajah."

"Well, we meet here at two. Say nothing about having seen me. I have a few odd things—a box or so—I should like to take with me.

"At two, Rajah," said Wakeling, walking away.

It was an unexpected bit of luck, falling in with this man.

Osric Grame had no longer need to hide his treasure. He could get away with it—go to Jamaica—and from thence speedily ship to anywhere. Once more fortune favoured him.

But he must take particular care not to be seen, and, to avoid observation, he walked along the beach as far as the in-tide permitted, and then climbing a cliff, sat down.

Suddenly he thought of Lina, and hastily looking about him, recognised the spot. It was the very place where he had bidden Pradu dispose of her.

Hurriedly rising, he walked further on, casting glances to the right and left, fearing to see some grim, midnight spectre.

Here and there he went, to kill the intervening time, not daring to show himself where he was likely to be seen, and suffering torture from superstitious fears.

At length the wished-for hour came, and returning to the appointed spot, he found Wakeling and two men awaiting him.

He showed them where the chests were, and told them a cock and bull story about them having all been kept in the cave, which Wakeling professed to believe.

It is not necessary to elaborately describe the work entailed in getting the chests on board the fishing-boat. It was successfully accomplished, there being nobody else abroad at that hour.

The vessel had scant accommodation of course.

There was a small cabin, with lockers on either side, which served as seats by day and sleeping-berths at night.

On one of them Osric Grame, worn out, lay down and speedily fell asleep.

When he awoke the sun was shining brightly, and, referring to his watch, he found it was ten o'clock.

As he sat up Wakeling came down and bade him good-morning.

"We thought we would not disturb you, Rajah," he said.

"It's all right," replied Osric Grame, "I am glad you did not. I wanted sleep. Where are we?"

"Forty miles from St. Marie," replied Wakeling, "sou'-west course, favourable wind. We have only rude fare, Rajah."

"Any fare will serve," replied Osric Grame.

Some herrings, potted meat, biscuits, and coffee were brought, and he partook of them alone.

At the top end of the cabin were his three treasure-chests piled one above another.

The locks worked without a key, but with a secret spring—which he had discovered shortly after they came into his possession.

All were of the same pattern, and he had no fear of the secret having been discovered by the crew of the boat until he had instructed them.

These springs were moved by pressing hard upon one of the nail-heads of the chests, just above the lock, and it had been his habit, after use, to rub some dirt or dust over them to hide the fact that they had a tendency to brighten, which arose from the action of pressing.

Looking at them now, he saw that the springs had been in recent action.

The nail-heads were quite bright, as if some inexperienced person had made several attempts to open the locks.

"These fellows have tried their hands at it," he muttered. "HAVE THEY SUCCEEDED !   Do they know what is inside !"

He went up to the deck, ostensibly to smoke and enjoy the sea-breeze, but really to scan the faces of the men, and, if possible, discover how much they knew.

Very little did he get for his pains.   There were no indications of the men having fathomed the secret of the chests, or of their taking any marked interest in him or his possessions.

Wakeling was talkative, and hinted two or three times that he would like to know why the Rajah wished to get away from St. Marie.

"You have so many friends there, Rajah," he said, "and they will miss you much."

"I may return among them by-and-bye," replied Osric Grame.   "How slowly this craft sails !"

"She is considered to be swift of her class," replied Wakeling.

Shortly after this conversation Osric Grame went below, and Wakeling a few minutes later followed him.

"Rajah," he said, "it seems to me that you are in a mighty hurry to get away from St. Marie, and I didn't quite make out what is in those boxes."

"Nothing but a few family relics," replied Osric.

"I'm fond of curiosities," said Wakeling, coolly ; "and if you don't mind, Rajah, I should like to see some of them."

"And if I refuse to show them ?"

"There are four to one of us, Rajah, and we shall look for ourselves."

"Perhaps you have seen already ?"

"No, Rajah.   I am no hand at lock-picking."

Osric Grame looked at him keenly.

The man appeared to be speaking the truth.

"Wakeling," he said, "I will trust YOU, but not the men. In ONE of these boxes there are jewels of considerable value—the others are full of rubbish. If you keep my secret I will reward you well as soon as I get ashore."

"Before," said Wakeling, calmly.

"Well, now," said Osric Grame, desperately. "You shall have a third of the contents of this box."

He rose up and touched the spring, standing with his back to Wakeling, so that the movement was hidden from him.

Raising the lid, he was about to draw Wakeling's attention to the contents, when a cry of dismay burst from him.

THE CHEST WAS FILLED WITH SAND AND STONES !

He tore it down and opened the second one.

The same !

Nothing in it but three or four big stones and some sand.

The third was also emptied of its original wealth and the worthless material substituted.

All three chests he had overturned, and the con-tents poured out upon the floor of the cabin.

Wakeling stared, but he knew nothing of the full portent of this discovery.

To Osric Grame it was a shock that almost killed him.

He stood over the rubbish for a few moments—dumb.

Then, raising his head, he stared wildly about him.

"ROBBED !" he shrieked—"ROBBED ! Who did it ? Wakeling—"

"How should I rob you ?" coolly asked Wakeling. "We brought the boxes aboard, and got away at once. How could we ha' done it ?"

"True—true," muttered Osric Grame ; "but who —WHO could have done it ? What witchcraft, what devilry, has been employed to BEGGAR me ?"

"If you haven't got any money," said Wakeling, "I am not going on to Jamaica. We must put about and return to St. Marie."

HAND me over that desk, Jack, please ; the time has come for me to read the 'True Story of John Amberton's Crime."

The two friends were in the cabin of the Water Sprite.

It was the evening following the departure of Osric Grame, and, having refused several courteous invitations to dine ashore, they were by choice alone.

In the course of the day they had been introduced to the governor, and met with a flattering reception, the way to it having been paved by Captain Fairfield.

"Dave," said Jack, "the time has come for mutual confidences, which might, perhaps, have been given before ; but we are neither of us curious or prying. Here is the desk."

Dave opened it and took out the paper which has been referred to before, and once more read the title—

"The True Story of John Amberton's Crime."

Unfolding the manuscript, he disclosed the fact that it was neatly and carefully written, and punctuated with the correctness of professional authorship.

"Shall I begin ?" asked Dave.

"I am ready," replied Jack, "as soon as I have lighted a cigar."

He put a match to one he held in his hand, drew at it two or three times, and added—

"Now fire away."

Dave leant back in his chair, and in a clear tone, with quiet force and a little appropriate dramatic action, read the following story—

"For many years nothing had caused so much sensation in the shires as the murder of Philip Amberton, one of the richest landowners in the north of England.

"I, the writer of these lines, am one of three sons born to him—the second in birth and the last in his affections. Ambrose was the eldest and Perrit the youngest son.

"Our mother died in giving Perrit birth, and as there was but a year between the children, none of us ever remembered a mother's care.

"The name of Philip Amberton stands high in the world of learning. He gave his time to his books and not to his children.

"Under the care of comparative strangers they grew up somewhat wild. Myself the wildest of all.

"Let me be frank.

"I can afford to be so, for I do not intend these lines to be read until I am dead, and I trust half the bitter record of my life forgotten. Let me be frank, I say, and admit that I was not only wild but vicious.

"Ambrose had no vice. He was a dashing, free-handed young fellow, and at twenty was a favourite with everybody around.

"With our father he stood foremost, and such time as he could spare from his books was given to him. Ambrose was his heir to the whole of the landed estates, while for the younger sons there was a fair amount of hard cash, the outcome of our father's economy.

"Perrit accepted this arrangement as a matter of course. I did not—I resented it—and in secret I resolved to get rid of Ambrose somehow, so that I, as the second son, might inherit all.

"Ambrose put a weapon into my hands by falling in love with a yeoman's daughter. He was honourable, and proposed marriage to her. She loved him, as everybody else did, and only my father's consent was wanted.

"He refused to give it, and violently reproached Ambrose for thinking of such a union.

"Ambrose left him, if not exactly in disgrace, at least, at variance with him, and being hot-tempered, went away, and within a week defiantly married the girl of his choice.

"Well! I thought I had gained my point then; but I had misjudged my father. He was bitterly angry for a time, but he soon forgave Ambrose, who came with his wife to live at the Pines, as our house was named.

"It was quite a family party, you see; but as neither Perrit nor myself were much at home we did not interfere with the arrangement.

"It was not, however, a happy settlement of the business. Words occasionally arose between Ambrose and my father, originating in a great measure in a little artful talk of mine—you see how frank I am—and a story got abroad that after all Ambrose would be disinherited.

"I put that story about, and there was not the

for certain that Philip Amberton had been murdered, stabbed in the back as he sat reading alone after dinner.

"His valet found him and gave the alarm. The police were sent for, and could find no trace of the murderer save what I gave them.

"I told them in confidence that I had seen Ambrose coming away from the study about half an hour before, looking pale and agitated.

"He was questioned on the subject and admitted he had been there, but solemnly declared that he and his father, so far from quarrelling, had become completely reconciled that night, and his agitation was the result of joy.

"They did not believe him—but I knew it was true, for I overheard what passed, and I saw all my hopes die away.

"There must be a devil in me somewhere, for I had never for a moment contemplated murder until that hour—nor did I contemplate it long then before I did it.

"Ambrose had not been gone a minute before I entered the room in a blind fury. On the wall hung a variety of weapons; for the most part curios collected abroad—among them a Damascus dagger.

"Possessed by a devil, I drew it from its sheath, struck at my father, and killed him. He never so much as uttered a groan.

"It was done, and I was not sorry.

"I exulted, because the flood of evil in my heart had been let loose. From that hour I was a lost man.

"Calmly I replaced the dagger and went to the billiard-room, where the butler found me quietly playing with Perrit when he sought us with what he called the ' awful news.'

" Awful news ! Not to me. I could have laughed, but I feigned sorrow and dismay, and I did my apparent best to bring the murderer to justice. I laugh even now as I think of it.

" Well, they arrested Ambrose and tried him for the murder. He was acquitted, because there was not sufficient in my evidence to convict him.

" But the stain was on him. Much as he was beloved, people could not believe he was innocent.

" I was loud in my protestations that he was guiltless. I declared my belief that his story was true, and, fearing to get suspicion on myself, set afloat all sorts of whispers about poor Perrit.

" He heard of them and came to me for advice. I counselled him to go abroad—he had inherited twenty thousand pounds—and live under an assumed name.

" I told him that nothing would shake the belief of the neighbours that he had committed the crime.

" He was an impulsive, ingenuous young fellow, on the verge of manhood, open to believe what he was told, and in despair he took another name and left England, as he told me, for ever.

" Then suspicion fell upon him ; but it never wholly left Ambrose, but rather fluctuated between them.

" Visitors deserted the Pines, the yeomen and poor people looked on Ambrose with doubting eyes, and when a child was born to him there was no public rejoicing, as there otherwise would have been.

" As our mother had died, so did the wife of Ambrose. It was a house of mourning. Tears of anguish hailed the new-born babe.

"Ah! it was a grand time for me and the devil within me. We enjoyed it hugely for awhile, and then Ambrose shut up the Pines and went away to the seaside, to live in quietude with his child.

"I wanted to go with him, to enjoy his misery, but he said 'No,' and came out with an unexpected declaration on his part.

"'John,' he said, 'I never was a man to encourage unjust suspicions, but I cannot quite shake off a feeling that our poor father died by your hand. I do not ask you to confess to me. The world is wide enough for us to live apart. Go away, and if this great sin be upon your head, strive to live a life of atonement. Repent, I beseech you, and pray for forgiveness.'

"I laughed in his face and went my way.

"His words had, however, alarmed me, and I hastened across the sea, choosing lone Nevada for my home.

"The devil within me now became rampant, and I degenerated into a fiend among men. They justly called me the Nevada Tiger.

"At last I became such a terror to men around that they made arrangements to dispose of me as they would have done with a dangerous wild beast.

"I heard of their project, and with two or three choice companions, who were sentenced to suffer with me, fled.

"It was then that I conceived the wild project of establishing piracy by cunning and mutiny.

"In New York I found the men to suit me, formed my company, and sent them, with qualified leaders, to join ships, and, at a fitting opportunity, murder their officers and bring their captures to the

"An old American sailor, who had been a pirate, told me of this most excellent haunt, and how far it has answered my purpose let the story of Osric Grame's success put on record.

"I have enjoyed many years of successful plunder, and lived the life of a monarch among my men.

"At intervals I have sent out letters addressed to my brother Ambrose, to be posted sometimes in one country, sometimes another—derisive letters mocking at his sufferings, and telling him stories of the life I have led. I even confessed that I murdered my father—only to add to his anguish.

"I am bad, utterly bad, hopelessly lost, chained to evil through time and eternity, and I can only find pleasure in giving pain.

"This is horribly frank, but I do not care how much you may hate me when I am gone.

"I ask for no man's love. Revile me now, and I ask no more. I have lived in evil, and I shall die in it. I am a man possessed.

"Having written this confession, I shall put it where it may one day be found—too late, I hope, for it to help my brother Ambrose.

"All I want is for the world to know what I have done, for I rejoice in my crimes, and would not recall any act of mine if it were in my power to do so.

"As a finale to this sketch, I may declare that luck goes with evil deeds. A paper has just come into my possession—it was found on board one of my captured ships—which, if it does not lie, makes me the master of many millions.

"Millions, in the hands of a man like me, mean much. If the paper be true, I shall return to the world, and play such havoc as wealth in the

CHAPTER XXXV.

MORE REVELATIONS—A LATE VISITOR—JACK GOES ASHORE.

 AVE had come to an end with his reading, and with a gesture expressive of loathing he tossed it into a corner of the cabin.

"What think you of that, Jack?" he asked.

"Horrible!—the man must be mad," was the answer.

"Yes, there is a madness of badness," said Dave; "it is a charitable interpretation to put upon his deeds, and now that I have read this paper you may ask of what interest it is to me?"

"I can almost guess it. You are—"

"The son of Ambrose Amberton, and my name s David. Now as to the identity of John Amberton—"

"That is clear. He and Osric Grame are one."

"It is true," said Dave, sadly, "and it is hard to have to hunt one's kith and kin as I have hunted him; but I have at home a father on whom the suspicion of murder has rested for twenty years. It has been his lingering hope that ere he died his good name would be restored. It has been my ambition from childhood to be the instrument of his social restoration.

"For that purpose," continued Dave, "I went early to sea, and, in the navy, studied the art of naval warfare. In the course of my life on board three or four warships I travelled to various parts of the world, grasping all the details of navigation,

unflagging in my zeal to imbibe all that could be
taught me. At an early age I left the navy and
pleaded with my father for the purchase of a suit-
able vessel wherewith to prosecute my search for
the man to whom so much misery is due."

"And by a miracle you have come upon his
track," said Jack.

"There are no miracles now-a-days," replied
Dave, "beyond the fact that life and all belonging
to it are a series of miracles. Everything is marvellous. From the first I have believed that success
would crown my quest; but I started under bad
auspices."

"How was that?"

"Our people at home got an inkling that I had
fitted out a vessel for some mysterious purpose,
and as at the same time whisperings of my uncle's
doings had reached the Admiralty it was assumed
that I had followed in his footsteps and taken to
nefarious pursuits upon the high seas. There are
even now war-ships looking for me and a price put
upon my head."

"But you will clear up matters Dave."

"Yes; I have done so with Fairfield, who knows
the history of my family, and in turn Sir Hercules
has been enlightened. As soon as possible he will
send home dispatches stating the facts of the case.
I shall be able to return home with honour as soon
as I have captured Osric Grame, alias John
Amberton.

"It is a strange story," said Jack, "a romance
deeper than mine. Strange to say, I too have suffered from a shadow arising from a crime cast upon
an innocent father. What it is I know not, but I
have seen since I was old enough to understand

how it has weighed upon him, burdening his life, embittering his waking hours, and giving him no rest save in the oblivion of sleep."

"And you are in search of a solution of the mystery ?"

" No ; not exactly. I never hoped for that. In time it began to weigh upon me too, and the unseen shadow made me miserable. I walked the earth, feeling that I was not as others and in a moment of more than usual restlessness, decided to go to sea. My father gave his consent. We were in America at the time, having wandered here and there for years. My mother—an American by birth—did not exactly approve, but she let me go. English instincts led me to serve my own country, but I took another name—that of Fenton. You found me, as you know, an ordinary seaman, took a fancy to me, and purchased my discharge. I have endeavoured to repay you by being faithful."

There was a strange, absent, wild light in Dave's eyes as he turned to Jack and said—

" There was more in our meeting than you as yet seem to guess. What was the name by which you knew your father ?"

" Powersley."

Dave got up from his seat and looked at him with tears standing in his eyes.

"Jack," he said, "we are of kindred blood— cousins. Powersley was the name assumed by Perrit Amberton when he left his native land."

Up to that moment Jack had never had a dim idea of there being any tie but that of friendship to bind them together ; but the few words uttered by Dave wiped away the whole mystery of his life.

For a few moments neither uttered a word.

With clasped hands they stood looking at each other, overcome with emotion. The whole thing was so startling, so overwhelming that for awhile it seemed as if they had been conversing in a dream ; but presently the mists of emotion began to clear away, and their whole history stood out like some picture in a powerful light.

"I will talk no more of chance," said Jack, "it was to be—IT IS.   Oh ! Dave it is a wonderful story of wrong and suffering, and the man who has caused it all—what of him ?"

"He must be found," said Dave, resolutely, "and for his crimes he must suffer. It would be a pity to be squeamish in dealing with him. He is allied by blood, but in nothing else. The man is hopelessly bad. He has been a scourge to us and all with whom he has come in contact. Were it possible for me to counsel mercy—could I see any good to come out of it—I would say : 'Let us go home and leave him.' But if we do so, we should be aiding and abetting him in his infamous career."

"Dave," said Jack, after a pause, "you have been my leader hitherto. Be my leader still. I will say no more."

"Be it so, Jack, but only for a little while. As the seers of old saw disaster marching down upon corrupt nations, so do I behold the steady descent of the sword of vengeance on that man."

"Have you any knowledge of where he is ?"

"No ; for the time he has eluded me ; but I know he schemes and hides in vain. The world is not big enough for him to escape me."

A tap at the door, the modest knock of Pegs, broke in upon their talk of strange events. He was bidden to come in.

"There's a man who wishes to see you, sir," he said to Dave.

"Who is he? What is he?"

"I don't know, sir. He looks like a fisherman, and he's come from the shore in a boat by himself."

"Send him down."

"Beg pardon, sir," said Pegs, "but I think an eye ought to be kept on him; he looks like a man not to be trusted."

"Have no fears," said Dave; "we will take good care that he does not surprise us."

Pegs with a doubtful air retired, and presently ushered in a half-caste in rough sea-going attire.

He saluted the cousins respectfully, and gave them "good-evening."

"Shall I wait, sir?" asked Pegs.

"No," replied Dave, "it is not necessary."

Pegs retired with a shake of the head which expressed much doubt of the worthiness of the half-caste.

Instead of going up, he lingered half way up to the deck—not to listen, but to be within call if anything untoward took place in the cabin.

Dave looked closely at the man. He was a roughish sort of fellow, but he did not look particularly dangerous. There was, on the contrary, a kindly gleam in his eye.

"You wished to speak to me?" said Dave.

"It is so, sare," was the reply. "I am about much. I hear—I know of your hatred of the Rajah."

"Well, my good fellow, that is hardly an affair of yours."

"No, sare, but you were kind to-day to my little lame boy. You see him in the street—you gave him money and soft words.   We half-breeds do not often get these things from your race."

"I believe I did see a little fellow creeping about the street," said Dave, "but I had almost forgotten the incident."

"I have not, I do not, and I shall not—for ever," said the man, "and I ask myself—'What shall I do for him who has been so kind to my boy—my little lame boy?'"

"I ask for nothing in return," said Dave.

"No, sare, but I see my way to do it. I hear from here and there that you want the Rajah. You look for him here. He is not here. He is gone."

Dave did not stir, but the news brought by the man was of great interest, and stirred his blood into quicker motion.

"What has become of him?" he asked.

"He has sailed away with Wakeling — fled. Pradu was to have gone with him, but he is dead. A bad man, and justly dead. No matter. It is not my affair of him."

"And what is the direction the Rajah, as you call him, has taken?"

"Ah! I know not exact," said the man, "but it was in the direction of Jamaica, or Cuba, one or other. The boat is slow. He has a long start, but your swift vessel could overtake him."

"Will you go with us?" asked Dave, quietly.

"Ah! I see you doubt," said the man, "you say to yourself—I will take this man, and if he has lied, I will hang him, the rascal! Sare, I am ready to go."

"No," said Dave, "I will trust you, for now I believe you to be honest. You may return home, and if I am successful in capturing Os— the Rajah, you shall be liberally rewarded."

"I will take nothing more," said the man. "Is it not enough, and more than enough, that you have been kind to my son—my little lame boy? Ah! we with the accursed black blood in us are not so flooded with kindness that we forget."

He touched his forehead, dashed out of the cabin, and closed the door.

As he bounded up the companion in the dark he ran against Pegs, who had not been quick enough to get out of his way.

"Stop a minute," said Pegs; "why this hurry? What have you been doing of?"

"Nothing," replied the man, "only trying to pay back the captain for his kindness to my son."

Pegs still held on, but voices in the cabin re-assured him and he set the man free.

"I suppose I ain't much of a judge of looks," he muttered, "for I could have sworn there was murder in YOUR eye."

In the cabin Dave and Jack were discussing the news they had heard. Dave was of opinion that it would not do to leave at once, but delay might enable Osric Grame (the old name comes most trippingly to the pen) to get away and give him a vast amount of trouble ere he was found again.

"Jack," he said, "I must go ashore and find Fair-field, so as to post him up with what we have heard. If he thinks Sir Hercules would not like me to leave, I must remain here. With the restoration of my father's good name virtually assured, the punish-ment of Osric Grame can wait."

"It seems to be decreed," replied Jack, "that the end of the fellow is to be a lingering one. I fancy

CHAPTER XXXVII.

THE HARVEST COMING IN—OSRIC AND HIS VICTIM —DOWN, DOWN TOGETHER.

ARELY in this world does a man escape reaping what he sows, and the harvest of Osric Grame, otherwise John Amberton, was drawing near.

He had returned to the island to seek for the treasure of which he considered he had been robbed.

Adverse winds delayed the return of the boat, and she had only succeeded in reaching St. Marie half an hour before.

As soon as the anchor was dropped he came ashore to find Andre Matadore, on whom he had fixed as the author of the "exchange trick" played upon him.

For hours he had tasted no strong drink, and his unstrung nerves twanged inharmoniously to every touch of the hand of self-reproach.

After moving about the island for some time, with no satisfactory result, he made up his mind to return on board for the present.

"I'll not stay here," he muttered. I am a fool! Why did I come at all?"

He turned towards the shore and came face to

Yes ; there was the form of the woman he had so bitterly injured, standing in a composed, graceful attitude a few feet from him.

At her feet lay a cloak, with which she had recently been covered. It had been useful to help her to disappear earlier in the evening.

It is a wonder he did not die from the shock the sight of her gave him.

He did not even stagger, but stood rooted to the spot, with the icy blasts of mental terror freezing is blood in his veins.

"Osric Grame," said the unexpectant visitant, "I see by your face that you think me dead ; but I am alive ! And I am here with you so that we may go on together to the end."

A sense of slowly-returning confidence came to his aid. He drew a long breath. Lina was not dead ! Ah ! that was something.

"I knew of your intention to drug me," she went on, "for I overheard you talking with that villain, Pradu, and the narcotic you intended to use was familiar to me. You have used it before. I also knew the antidote, and prepared myself to thwart you. The drug you gave me was powerless."

Again he drew a deep breath, but said nothing.

"Shamming unconsciousness," pursued Lina, "I allowed you to thrust me into the sack for your confederate to shoot me over the cliff. Bah ! what a mean, cowardly trick. You were afraid to kill me with your own hand, so you would have stupefied me and left a bolder villain to finish the business. I had everything ready, and thrust a dummy figure into the sack after I had crept out again. I saw Pradu bear the sham victim to the precipice and shoot it over. It made me laugh. For the first time for many a year I had a moment of merriment. But it soon passed, and I prepared myself to be your bane. Do you hear me?"

"Yes," he answered, in a crushed voice.

"I hid myself in yon cave, where I afterwards saw you and your boon companion steal away with your recovered treasure. Again I had a moment of merriment, and that was something for me to enjoy. Osric Grame, it was I WHO robbed you."

"Ah!" he exclaimed, "it was you—hag!"

"Be composed," she said, quietly, "I am not afraid of you. Threats would be wasted on me. I do not fear you. And I pray you remember what I said. I am here to go with you—to the end."

"If that is so, Lina," he said, in a low tone, "I forgive you."

She smiled in a strange way; but her face was in the shadow, and he did not see it.

"With money," he went on, "we may be happy even now. Surely, we can forget the past."

"Can we?" she asked. "Would that I could forget! But not in this world. As for our being happy—do you forget that I am OLD—that in years, young, I am in looks a HAG?"

"Yes," he answered with a groan.

"And it was YOUR work," said Lina. "You made me what I am. Ah! what a hell you have made my life. And do you remember what I was when you lured me away from my home in Nevada—an innocent, trustful girl?"

"Yes—yes," he interposed; "but I cannot give you back what you have lost. I will try to make amends in the future. Where is my wealth?"

"Not far from here," she answered. "Come with me."

He followed her eagerly with renewed life, and the black determination in his heart to kill her the moment she revealed the hiding-place of the jewels.

"We will never part again," she said, looking back at him.

"No," he said, "never.'

"It shall be so," she rejoined ; "we go on now to the end."

She glided on, muttering to herself, "To the end —to the end," and he, with his thoughts absorbed in the prospect of recovering what he had lost failed to mark her words.

On, across the garden, first to the spot by the fountain, where the sack, supposed to contain her inanimate body, had lain that night, and then on by the track Pradu had taken, across a rugged piece of ground to the verge of the cliff.

Then she faced around.

"It was here," she said, "that your accomplice came that night—to put an end to me."

"Well, let us forget all that," replied Osric Grame. "Where are my jewels ?"

"Come and see them," she answered ; "just there—by yon rocks below—within that cave."

He stepped forward and eagerly peered over the cliff, to mark the spot she pointed out.

The next moment she was upon him.

With hands that were fastened upon him like claws, a tigress had attacked the Tiger of Nevada.

"To the end !" she shrieked, "we go together !"

Her voice rang out sharp and shrill upon the night air. Two answering cries were heard by Osric Grame, battling with a wild woman for his

He knew those voices—one was Daring Dave's, the other was that of Andre Matadore.

They came up from two different directions, within sight of each other and of the man and woman on the verge of the cliff, at the same moment.

Appalled, and helpless to save they both stopped, spell-bound watchers of the dreadful scene.

A moment later Captain Fairfield had joined Dave.

"Help—help !"

It was Osric Grame, who, in the terror of his last moments, cried out for aid.

He sought help of those whom he had wronged and bitterly treated, and the moment the cry escaped him a sense of humiliation came over him.

What would he have given to recall that appeal for help ?

But he had nothing to give, no opportunity for giving.

With the strength of a man and the tenacity of a tigress, Lina clung to him, dragging herself with him inch by inch to the edge of the cliff.

Only a short journey, a foot or so, and vain was his effort to avoid his fate.

Even when he at length got a firm foothold, and a good grip on the maddened Lina, now truly mad, the soil beneath him came to the aid of his enemies.

The edge of the cliff broke away, and plunging forward, Osric Grame and his victim, Lina, rushed headlong together down, to be literally dashed to pieces on the rocks below.

CHAPTER XXXVIII.

ADIEU.

THE tide was out, and when lights and assistance were procured, the witnesses of the dreadful scene hurried round to see what could be done for the fallen.

It was not a sight for sensitive men, and it made the strong ones shudder. Though mangled in body by the awful fall, Lina with her hands still grasped the clothing of the man she had suffered so much for. In one mad act she had avenged the torture of years.

"Let them be buried together," said Dave, "in some place where the very spot will be forgotten."

His wishes were carried out.

There was a rough form of inquest on the following day. A suicide's grave was apportioned to both.

They were buried when the tide was out among the rocks, and there left to be, in time, forgotten.

A search was made for the missing treasure, and it was discovered in the cave Lina pointed out to Osric Grame.

So far she had been truthful.

Daring Dave refused to touch any of it.

He had enough, and more than enough, for himself, and those who had shared his adventurous cause upon the sea, and it was handed over to Captain Fairfield.

"It is right that you should have it," said Daring Dave, "for without your aid Osric Grame might have triumphed after all."

"You are more than generous," said Captain Fairfield. "I won't be quixotic in the matter. The fortune is welcome, for I am poor, and I have a wife at home. My chance of getting another ship is very small, for the Admiralty never forgive an unavoidable accident. A stupid blunder is more readily pardoned."

Daring Dave and Fiery Jack were both anxious to get home, and a few days later the Water Sprite set sail.

It is no figure of speech when we declare that every inhabitant of St. Marie came to give her a parting cheer, which meant a long course of hurrahs.

The response from the Water Sprite was hearty, but high above all sounds was heard that wonderful musical instrument which Vunder Fule played so well.

He started with the first cheer, beginning with the overture to the "Vinkle and the Vhale," and succeeded in getting more than half through it ere the cheery shouts had ceased.

Then, on his appealing to be allowed to finish it, Daring Dave gave his consent, and immediately dived below, followed by Fiery Jack.

Pegs, Crupper, and the seamen put tow in their ears, and manfully bore the rest of the infliction.

.   .   .   .

Our story has virtually come to an end.

The Water Sprite got safely home, arriving in a dismantled condition, as far as her guns were concerned.

They were stowed below, there being no further need of them. In a peaceful garb she dropped her anchor in British waters.

Long before this each man on board had received his share of the pirate's spoil, and to a man they had decided to have the proceeds invested so as to make them all comfortable for life.

The greater part of the treasure was, of course, divided between Jack and Dave.

Vunder Fule decided to buy a cottage somewhere in the country, where he could study music, compose operas, and play them in peace.

Crupper recommended the middle of Salisbury Plain, but as there was no cottage in that lone district Vunder Fule did not go thither.

For Jack there was the welcome of friends ; to Dave that of a father, whose brow, deep-furrowed with grief and care, was smoothed out by the tidings of his son's success.

Both are married now, each with a little family of his own, living in Leicestershire, where Daring Dave still keeps his name owing to his plucky riding, and Fiery Jack retains his, thanks to his impetuosity on horseback, which often lands him in a ditch or brook.

It is the same with the youngsters ; the eldest, Dave's son, is only ten, but he goes about on a half wild Shetland pony as if there were no possibility of being dislodged from the saddle.

Crupper and Pegs live together down by the sea, and once a year Vunder Fule pays them a visit, bringing with him that marvellous instrument.

Each eve during his stay he is allowed to " blow up" five minutes after sundown, and he does it in a style that makes the natives sit up and—well, say something we do not mean to put in print.

The crew of the Water Sprite have scattered here and there, as men are apt to do in this world of ours ; but as no ill-tidings of any of them have as yet come to hand, we assume that they are all happy and well.

And so, with the work of one and all done, and well done, we take leave of the gallant hearts of the Water Sprite and their noble leader, Daring Dave.

It was many years after the chief event of our story when a ship, driven out of her course, anchored off the island where Osric Grame once lived in infamous retirement.

Some of the sailors went ashore for water, and one of them, armed with a gun, came across what he believed to be a huge baboon.

He shot the creature dead upon the spot, and two minutes afterwards discovered it was a MAN.

It was Lacroix, the sole survivor of the three men left on the island.

Waydown Bubbs and Nozzle had died in misery years before, and their bones lay bleaching on the sandy shore.

THE END.

ALL VOLUMES ARE IN STOCK.

THREEPENNY COMPLETE VOLUMES.

DARING DAVE;
OR, THE TREASURES OF THE DEEP.

THE BRIGANDS OF PALESTRA

A BOY OF A THOUSAND.

FOOTBALL IN COKETOWN; OR,
WHO SHALL BE CAPTAIN?

THE CHING CHING MYSTERY.

THE WILD ADVENTURES OF
EDDARD & JAM JOSSER ABROAD.

THE WILD ADVENTURES OF
EDDARD & JAM JOSSER AT HOME.

THE FURTHER EXPLOITS
OF EDDARD AND JAM JOSSER.

THE SLAPCRASH BOYS;
THE LIVELIEST OF SCHOOL STORIES.

JACK CŒUR DE LION:
OUTCAST AND HERO.

MAJOR NIGHTMARE OF CAMP
CLIMAX.

THE MESMERIST DETECTIVE:
OR, STRANGE DOINGS IN LITTLEWOOD.

PLUCKY PHIL FARREN; OR, THE
MYSTERY OF BRYTHEWAITE SCHOOL.

HAL O' THE HEATH,
THE WANDERING HEIR.

THE BRAND OF THE BLACK STAR.

LIONEL THE BOLD; OR, THE
CIRCUS RIDER'S REVENGE.

VALIANT ROY; OR, THE PIRATE'S
SCOURGE.

SIXPENNY COMPLETE VOLUMES.

JACK JAUNTY,
THE HERO OF SEAGULL CLIFF.

DAUNTLESS DONALD DREW; OR,
BESET BY BITTER FOES.

RADDLETON ROCKET'S ROVING
SCHOOLBOYS.

THE ADVENTURES OF
BOLD BEN BRIERTON AND TINY
TIMOTHY TOPPEM.

OUR BOYS ABROAD;
OR, THE BLACK BANDITS OF THE
RHINE

CHING CHING AND HIS CHUMS;
A MIRTHFUL, MOVING, AND
MYSTERIOUS STORY.

JACK OF THE GOLDEN BELT;
OR, STIRRING ADVENTURES IN THE
SWAMPS OF CUBA.

YOUNG CHING AT SCHOOL;
OR, HIGH OLD TIMES FOR THE
SLAPCRASHERS.

DARING CHING CHING;
OR, THE MYSTERIOUS CRUISE OF THE
SWALLOW.

GALLANT HAL AND THE CREW
OF THE SILVER STAR.

THE VEILED CAPTAIN;
OR, THE HERO OF EAGLE CRAIG.

DICK STORNAWAY;
OR, A HERO IN SPITE OF HIS FOES.

THE BANGWELL BOYS.

ONE SHILLING COMPLETE VOLUMES.

HARDIBOY JAMES:
OR, CHUMS AND CHAPPIES

HANDSOME HARRY OF THE
FIGHTING BELVEDERE. Vols. I. & II.

CHEERFUL CHING CHING; THE
SEQUEL TO "HANDSOME HARRY."

TOM TARTAR AT SCHOOL. Vols. I. & II.

DICK STRONGBOW, THE WONDER
OF THE WORLD. Vols. I. & II

WONDERFUL CHING CHING.

YOUNG CHING CHING. Vols. I. & II.

TWO SHILLING COMPLETE VOLUMES.

DICK STRONGBOW, THE WONDER OF THE WORLD.

YOUNG CHING CHING.   TOM TARTAR AT SCHOOL.

HANDSOME HARRY OF THE FIGHTING BELVEDERE.

'BEST FOR BOYS' PUBLISHING CO., 17, GOUGH SQUARE, FLEET-ST., LONDON.

www.ingramcontent.com/pod-product-compliance
Lightning Source LLC
Chambersburg PA
CBHW080732250626
47170CB00010B/2803